MW00574240

Genesis
Deflowered

MATTHEW STILLMAN

Genesis Deflowered © 2013 Matthew Stillman

All rights reserved. No part of this book may be reproduced in any form
or by any electronic or mechanical means, including information storage
and retrieval systems, without permission from the publisher, except by a
reviewer, who may quote brief passages in a review. Scanning, uploading,
and electronic distribution of this book or the facilitation of such without the
permission of the publisher is prohibited. Please purchase only authorized
electronic editions, and do not participate in or encourage electronic piracy
of copyrighted materials. Your support of the author's rights is appreciated.
Any inquiries should be directed to m@stillmansays.com.

First published in the United States of America by Sheffield Moors Press,
New York.

ISBN - 978-0-9896968-0-7

Author: Matthew Stillman
Editor: Veronica Tuggle
Book Cover Design: Jane Dixon-Smith
Book Layout Design: Jane Dixon-Smith

Contents

Acknowledgements

This book would not be possible without my weird friend, Jill Hamilton, who inadvertently sent me down the path of writing this book. And it certainly would not have been possible without discovering my brilliant, tenacious, and insightful editor Veronica Tuggle, whom I found in the most wonderful and mysterious way. She was the perfect editor and made the book better with every single correction and suggestion she made. I am so grateful to her. And, of course, to Susan. She is the very best.

A Note to the Reader

"*Genesis Deflowered*" is written in the literary style of the King James Bible, Cambridge Edition.

The King James Version of the Bible was written during the Jacobean era by Elizabethan era writers and poets, so although the usage is modern English, it is early modern, not current.

Because of this, things like "help meet" and "An hundred" sound dissonant to our ears, but they are within the style of the times. While we blanch at starting almost every sentence with "and", this was a common technique during that time.

Our job, as author and editor, was to mirror the style of the original text so that the new text fits in with the old. Part of that process was to take those same strange features of writing and dialogue, such as never using quotation marks, and use them as if they were our own.

If you were to cross-reference the areas you believe are mistakes or typographical errors with an online version of the King James Bible, you may be surprised to see that, to our modern eyes, the Bible itself seems to be filled with errors in spelling, punctuation, and grammar. These are not actually errors. They are merely differences in style that have changed over time.

The Creation

n the beginning God created the heaven and the earth. And the earth was without form, and void; and darkness was upon the face of the deep. As the face of God touched the face of the deep, their ardour grew for each other. And the Spirit of God moved upon the face of the waters. And the Hand of The Spirit of God held the fair face of the water with a yearning to create.

And God said, Let there be light: and there was light. And God saw the light, that it was good: and God divided the light from the darkness. And God called the light Day, and the darkness he called Night. And the evening and the morning were the first day.

The ardour to create more rose in God. And God said, Let there be a firmament in the midst of the waters, and let it divide the waters from the waters. And God made the firmament, and he held it closely unto him. Then he divided the waters which were under the firmament from the waters which were above the firmament: and it was so. And God called the firmament Heaven. And the evening and the morning were the second day.

And God delighted in the touch of his creation. And God said, Let the waters under the heaven be gathered together unto one place, and let the dry land appear: and it was so. And God called the dry land Earth; and the gathering together of the waters called he Seas: and God saw that it was good. And God said, Let the earth bring forth grass, the herb yielding seed, and the fruit tree yielding fruit after his kind, whose seed is in itself, upon the earth: and it was so. And the earth brought forth grass, and herb yielding seed after his kind, and the tree yielding fruit, whose seed was in itself, after his kind. And he knew of the desire of the seed to spread itself on dry land, and in the waters called Seas: and God saw that it was good. And he saw the desire, and blessed it. And the evening and the morning were the third day.

And God said, Let there be lights in the firmament of the heaven to divide the day from the night; and let them be for signs, and for seasons, and for days, and years, and lovings: And let them be for lights in the firmament of the heaven to give light upon the earth: and it was so. And God made two great lights; the greater light to rule the day, and the lesser light to rule the night: he made the stars also. In his hands, the lights shone, and warmed the face of God. And God set them in the firmament of the heaven to give light upon the earth, And to rule over the day and over the night, and to divide the light from the darkness: and God saw that it was good. And the evening and the morning were the fourth day.

And God said, Let the waters bring forth abundantly the moving creature that hath life, and fowl that may fly above the earth in the open firmament of heaven. And God created great whales, and every living creature that moveth, which the waters brought forth abundantly, after their kind, and every winged fowl after his kind: and God saw that it was good. And God blessed them, saying, Be fruitful, and multiply, and fill the waters in the seas, and let fowl multiply in the earth. And so all the moving creatures, like the grasses before them, knew the desire to spread their seed, so that they might be fruitful and multiply; and God saw that it was good. And God saw this desire, and blessed it. And the evening and the morning were the fifth day.

And God said, Let the earth bring forth the living creature after his kind, cattle, and creeping thing, and beast of the earth after his kind: and it was so. And God made the beast of the earth after his kind, and cattle after their kind, and every thing that creepeth upon the earth after his kind: and God saw that, lo, like the grass and the creatures that move, they also longed to spread their seed. And God knew this desire in himself, and saw that it was good.

And God said, Let us make man in our image, after our likeness: and let them have dominion over the fish of the sea, and over the fowl of the air, and over the cattle, and over all the earth, and over every creeping thing that creepeth upon the earth. Let him be steward and caretaker. So God created man in his own image; creator, lover, and caretaker, in the image of God created he him; male and female created he them. And God blessed them, and God said unto them, Be fruitful, and multiply, know the ardour I had for the waters and the face of the deep. Know the desire of the grass, the moving creatures, and the beasts. Know them to be good, and replenish the earth, and subdue it: and have dominion over the fish of the sea, and over the fowl of the air, and over every living thing that moveth upon the earth. Care for each as I have cared for and formed each day.

And God said, Behold, I have given you every herb bearing seed, which is upon the face of all the earth, and every tree, in which is the fruit of a tree yielding seed; to you it shall be for meat. And to every beast of the earth, and to every fowl of the air, and to every thing that creepeth upon the earth, wherein there is life, I have given every green herb for meat: and it was so. And God saw every thing that he had made, and behold, as man and woman learnt to spread their seed to each other, and yea it was very good. And the evening and the morning were the sixth day.

Thus the heavens and the earth were finished, and all the host of them. And on the seventh day God ended his work which he had made; and he rested on the seventh day from all his work which he had made. And God blessed the seventh day, and sanctified it: because that in it he had rested from all his work which God created and made.

The Garden of Eden

hese are the generations of the heavens and of the earth when they were created, in the day that the LORD God made the earth and the heavens. And every plant of the field before it was in the earth, and every herb of the field before it grew: for the LORD God had not caused it to rain upon the earth, and there was not a man to till the ground. But there went up a mist from the earth, and watered the whole face of the ground. And the LORD God formed man of the dust of the ground, and breathed into his nostrils the breath of life; and man became a living soul, with a desire to spread seed like the grass, the moving creatures, and the beasts.

And the LORD God planted a garden eastward in Eden; and there he put the man whom he had formed. And out of the ground made the LORD God to grow every tree that is pleasant to the sight, and good for food; the tree of life also in the midst of the garden, and the tree of knowledge of good and evil. And a river, parted from the Seas by God, went out of Eden to water the garden; and from thence it was parted, and became into four heads. The name of the first is Pison: that is it which compasseth the whole land of Havilah, where there is gold; And the gold of that land is good: there is bdellium and the onyx stone. And God knew that the gold and bdellium and onyx were to be given as offerings of love between his creations. And the name of the second river is Gihon: the same is it that compasseth the whole land of Ethiopia. And the name of the third river is Hiddekel: that is it which goeth toward the east of Assyria. And the fourth river is Euphrates.

And the LORD God took the man, and put him into the garden of Eden to dress it and to keep it. And the LORD God commanded the man, saying, Of every tree of the garden thou mayest freely eat: But of the tree of the knowledge of good and evil, thou shalt not eat of it: for in the day that thou eatest thereof thou shalt surely die.

And the LORD God said, It is not good that the man should be alone; I will make him an help meet for him. And out of the ground the LORD God formed every beast of the field, and every fowl of the air; and brought them unto Adam to see what he would call them: and whatsoever Adam called every living creature, that was the name thereof. And Adam gave names to all cattle, and to the fowl of the air, and to every beast of the field; but for Adam there was not found an help meet for him.

And the LORD God caused a deep sleep to fall upon Adam and he slept: and he took one of his ribs closest to his heart, and closed up the flesh instead thereof; And the rib, which the LORD God had taken from man, made he a woman, and brought her unto the man. And Adam said, This is now bone of my bones, and flesh of my flesh: she shall be called Woman, because she was taken out of Man.

Therefore shall a man leave his father and his mother, and shall cleave unto his wife: and they shall be one flesh. And they were both naked, the man and his wife, and were not ashamed as they showed each to the other the firmness of their lands, and the wetness of their seas. They supped upon each other as if for foods. And the LORD God watched the sea swallow the land; and he saw that it was good.

The Expulsion from Eden

ow the serpent was more subtil than any beast of the field which the LORD God had made. And he said unto the woman, Yea, hath God said, Ye shall not eat of every tree of the garden?

And the woman said unto the serpent, We may eat of the fruit of the trees of the garden and of each other, as if for food: But of the fruit of the tree which is in the midst of the garden, God hath said, Ye shall not eat of it, neither shall ye touch it, lest ye die. And the serpent said unto the woman, Ye shall not surely die: For God doth know that in the day ye eat thereof, then your eyes shall be opened, and ye shall be as gods, knowing good and evil. And when the woman saw that the tree was good for food, and that it was pleasant to the eyes, and a tree to be desired to make one wise, she took of the fruit thereof, and did eat, and gave also unto her husband with her; and he did eat. And the eyes of them both were opened, and they knew that they were naked; and they sewed fig leaves together, and made themselves aprons. And they heard the voice of the LORD God walking in the garden in the cool of the day: and Adam and his wife hid themselves from the presence of the LORD God amongst the trees of the garden.

And the LORD God called unto Adam, and said unto him, Where art thou? And he said, I heard thy voice in the garden, and I was afraid, because I was naked; and I hid myself. And he said, Who told thee that thou wast naked? Hast thou eaten of the tree, whereof I commanded thee that thou shouldest not eat? And the man said, The woman whom thou gavest to be with me, she gave me of the tree, and I did eat. And the LORD God said unto the woman, What is this that thou hast done? And the woman said, The serpent beguiled me, and I did eat.

And the LORD God said unto the serpent, Because thou hast done this, thou art cursed above all cattle, and above every beast of the field; upon thy belly shalt thou go, and dust shalt thou eat all the days of thy life: And I will put enmity between thee and the woman, and between thy seed and her seed; it shall bruise thy head, and thou shalt bruise his heel. Unto the woman he said, For I have sorrow at this, and now so must you. I will greatly multiply thy sorrow and thy conception; in sorrow thou shalt bring forth children; and thy desire shall be to thy husband, and he shall rule over thee. And unto Adam he said, Because thou hast hearkened unto the voice of thy wife, and hast eaten of the tree, of which I commanded thee, saying, Thou shalt not eat of it: cursed is the ground for thy sake; in sorrow shalt thou eat of it all the days of thy life; Thorns also and thistles shall it bring forth to thee; and thou shalt eat the herb of the field; In the sweat of thy face shalt thou eat bread, till thou return unto the ground; for out of it wast thou taken: for dust thou art, and unto dust shalt thou return.

But I have made thee with love; and thou art but like children unto me; thus not all is a curse for thee. In the day, and in the night, when thou rememberest my love and desire, and makest it thine own, and forgettest thy nakedness, lo, will my curse be lifted; and for that while, thou shalt return to this garden. But after, yea, this curse shall return upon thee.

And Adam called his wife's name Eve; because she was the mother of all living. Unto Adam also and to his wife did the LORD God make coats of skins, and clothed them. And the LORD God said, Behold, the man is become as one of us, to know good and evil: and now, lest he put forth his hand, and take also of the tree of life, and eat, and live for ever: Therefore the LORD God sent him forth from the garden of Eden, to till the ground from whence he was taken. So he drove out the man; and he placed at the east of the garden of Eden Cherubim, and a flaming sword which turned every way, to keep the way of the tree of life.

Cain and Abel

nd Adam knew Eve his wife, as if for the first time. The curse of the LORD God was lifted as Adam lifted the skins upon his wife Eve, and gazed upon her nakedness. And she held tightly upon his stem, and licked his breast with great hunger, as the bee licks the blossom. Then Adam bound Eve in his arms; and their secrets cleaved unto each other. Their seed knew each other; and they knew the garden for that day. And from this, she conceived, and bare Cain, and said, I have gotten a man from the LORD.

And she again shared her nakedness with Adam. She held tightly upon his staff; and the staff stood for the waters. Adam bared his breast in his desire for Eve. And he entered her thighs in his mount; and they both knew the garden together. In time, she bare Cain's brother Abel.

And Abel was a keeper of sheep, but Cain was a tiller of the ground. And in process of time it came to pass, that Cain brought of the fruit of the ground an offering unto the LORD. And Abel, he also brought of the firstlings of his flock and of the fat thereof. And the LORD had respect unto Abel and to his offering: But unto Cain and to his offering he had not respect. And Cain was very wroth, and his countenance fell.

And the LORD said unto Cain, Why art thou wroth? and why is thy countenance fallen? If thou doest well, shalt thou not be accepted? and if thou doest not well, sin lieth at the door. And unto thee shall be his desire, and thou shalt rule over him. And Cain talked with Abel his brother: and it came to pass, when they were in the field, that Cain rose up against Abel his brother, and slew him with the iron piece of his plough. And the blood of Abel was spilt upon the earth and it streamed before his flock.

And the LORD said unto Cain, Where is Abel thy brother? And he said, I know not: Am I my brother's keeper? And he said, What hast thou done? the voice of thy brother's blood crieth unto me from the ground. And now art thou cursed from the earth, which hath opened her mouth to receive thy brother's blood from thy hand; When thou tillest the ground, it shall not henceforth yield unto thee her strength; a fugitive and a vagabond shalt thou be in the earth. And Cain said unto the LORD, My punishment is greater than I can bear. Behold, thou hast driven me out this day from the face of the earth; and from thy face shall I be hid; and I shall be a fugitive and a vagabond in the earth; and it shall come to pass, that every one that findeth me shall slay me. And the LORD said unto him, Therefore whosoever slayeth Cain, vengeance shall be taken on him sevenfold. And the LORD set a mark upon Cain, lest any finding him should kill him. And Cain was now the bad son.

And Cain went out from the presence of the LORD, and dwelt in the land of Nod, on the east of Eden. His sin and his wroth drew the desire of his wife; for the mark summoned desire. And his wife was called Ishshah. And Cain knew Ishshah. In his wroth he gnashed his teeth as his heel entered the waters. And his wife wailed with the dust betwixt her joys; and her hair hung low and wild. And his hand bore into her secrets. And his wife kept his heel as the seas rose. She clasped his mark; and they saw the garden. She conceived, and bare Enoch: and he builded a city, and called the name of the city, after the name of his son, Enoch. And unto Enoch was born Irad: and Irad begat Mehujael: and Mehujael begat Methusael: and Methusael begat Lamech.

And Lamech took unto him two wives: the name of the one was Adah, and the name of the other Zillah. And in the tent they lay with each other. Lamech upon his knees knew the secrets of Adah. And Zillah delighted in the breast of Adah, as Lamech took the plow to the fertile land of Adah. And the liver of Adah shook, as they saw the garden together; and the seeds of Lamech scattered in the land of Adah. Then Zillah came upon Adah, and tasted of her mouth and polished neck, and found her secret with her hand. And by her hand did they journey to the garden. Lamech touched the faces of Adah and Zillah, and then he rested. And Zillah parted the thighs of Adah, and tasted of her nakedness until they saw the garden. And Zillah woke Lamech, so that she might be filled for her hunger. And Zillah and Adah hid the rod amidst their breasts, and drank of the staff of Lamech, as he anointed them. Lamech pressed into the waters of the land of Zillah, and scattered his seed there. And that night Lamech and Adah and Zillah rested together in the garden.

And Adah bare Jabal: he was the father of such as dwell in tents, and of such as have cattle. And his brother's name was Jubal: he was the father of all such as handle the harp and organ. And Zillah, she also bare Tubal-cain, an instructer of every artificer in brass and iron: and the sister of Tubal-cain was Naamah. And Lamech said unto his wives, Adah and Zillah, Hear my voice; ye wives of Lamech, hearken unto my speech: for I have slain a man to my wounding, and a young man to my hurt. If Cain shall be avenged sevenfold, truly Lamech seventy and sevenfold.

And Adam was full of lamentations for the death of his son Abel. And in his grief he knew his wife Eve again. In tears did he place his face upon hers. And in sorrow and with working woe did they care for the thighs of the other. And in the long quiet dark did they remember Abel. No tears did flow; for in their breath did they know his death. They tended to the garden; and she bare a son, and called his name Seth: For God, said she, hath appointed me another seed instead of Abel, whom Cain slew. And to Seth, to him also there was born a son; and he called his name Enos: then began men to call upon the name of the LORD.

The Descendants of
Adam and Eve

his is the book of the generations of Adam and Eve. In the day that God created man, in the likeness of God made he him; Male and female created he them; and blessed them, and called their name Adam and Eve, in the day when they were created.

And Adam lived an hundred and thirty years, and begat a son in his own likeness, after his image; and called his name Seth: And the days of Adam after he had begotten Seth were eight hundred years: and he begat sons and daughters: And all the days that Adam lived were nine hundred and thirty years: and he died. And Seth lived an hundred and five years, and begat Enos: And Seth lived after he begat Enos eight hundred and seven years, and begat sons and daughters: And all the days of Seth were nine hundred and twelve years: and he died.

And Enos lived ninety years, and begat Cainan: And Enos lived after he begat Cainan eight hundred and fifteen years, and begat sons and daughters: And all the days of Enos were nine hundred and five years: and he died.

And Cainan lived seventy years, and begat Mahalaleel: And Cainan lived after he begat Mahalaleel eight hundred and forty years, and begat sons and daughters: And all the days of Cainan were nine hundred and ten years: and he died.

And Mahalaleel lived sixty and five years, and begat Jared: And Mahalaleel lived after he begat Jared eight hundred and thirty years, and begat sons and daughters: And all the days of Mahalaleel were eight hundred ninety and five years: and he died.

And Jared lived an hundred sixty and two years, and he begat Enoch: And Jared lived after he begat Enoch eight hundred years, and begat sons and daughters: And all the days of Jared were nine hundred sixty and two years: and he died.

And Enoch lived sixty and five years, and begat Methuselah: And Enoch walked with God after he begat Methuselah three hundred years, and begat sons and daughters by Edna the daughter of Danel. And Enoch made Edna conceive by his hot breath; and Edna took his breath to her womb; and did give back breath to Enoch in kind. And that breath did rise up their backs, each unto each, making a whirlwind of joy that did blow them to the gates of the garden: And all the days of Enoch were three hundred sixty and five years: And Enoch walked with God in one heavenly circle: and he was not; for God took him for his righteousness, to spare him death.

And Methuselah lived an hundred eighty and seven years, and begat Lamech: And Methuselah lived after he begat Lamech seven hundred eighty and two years, and begat sons and daughters: And all the days of Methuselah were nine hundred sixty and nine years: and he died.

And Lamech lived an hundred eighty and two years, and wifed Betenos. Betenos sped to Lamech, yearning for her thighs to be known by him. And her hair was dark like the raven, and flowed like rivers. Lamech did walk upon the earth with a staff made of olive branch, and bearing beads of mastic as gifts to Betenos. And their mouths did become one mouth; and their breasts did become one breast. And the olives of Lamech did oil the river of Betenos. And the waters of Betenos did crest and roll. And she knew the garden for many nights, and was comforted. And she begat a son by Lamech: And he called his name Noah, saying, This same shall comfort us concerning our work and toil of our hands, because of the ground which the LORD hath cursed. And Lamech lived after he begat Noah five hundred ninety and five years, and begat sons and daughters: And all the days of Lamech were seven hundred seventy and seven years: and he died.

And Noah was five hundred years old: and Noah begat Shem, Ham, and Japheth.

And it came to pass, when men began to multiply on the face of the earth, and daughters were born unto them, That the sons of God saw the daughters of men that they were fair; and they took them wives of all which they chose. And the sons of God did forget to always be kind to the daughters, and to let they themselves be chosen, by and by. For God is the LORD of comings, but also of goings. So, as he is the river that flows, so is he the jar that dips into it and keeps the waters still. And the LORD said, My spirit shall not always strive with man, for that he also is flesh: yet his days shall be an hundred and twenty years.

There were giants in the earth in those days at the height of three men. And four daughters would come together to act as one woman, and to meet and satisfy one giant for his sake. Daughters bound to daughters by strap, and cord, and bridle, and tack, so that one and three of mouths became one great mouth, and twice four breasts, and one great womb made of four. And the daughters danced round about, with reed pipes and tabors, and drank of rich draughts for loving and for strength. And all about did cheer, and dance and sing in kind. And the giant of the earth did kiss the four mouths as one. And the daughters did kiss back in their hungers. The daughters sat athwart the staff of the giant, anointing the staff of the giant with their thighs. And each daughter sat at the head of the staff to receive the blessing of the giant. And they bare children to him.

And the giant daughter at the height of three women had three and one of the sons bind themselves together by strap, and cord, and bridle, and tack and act as one man. For the giant daughter needed her satisfactions unto the LORD. And the four men did lift the skins of the giant daughter, and did taste of the waters and pressed with hands upon her walls. The breasts of the daughter were tended by two sons, and two others kissed upon the mouth of the beautiful giant. And the men made a team of four in a line down the front of the giantess. And the men from three different roads did bring the giant daughter to the garden. And all around played trumpets of silver, and frame drums made of cypress as she made her way into the garden. And they did make a pot for all seeds; and the pot was emptied into the womb of the daughter. Lo, the daughters bare children unto them, the same became mighty as well.

And also after that, when the sons of God came in unto the daughters of men, and they bare children to him, the same became mighty men which were of old, men of renown.

But the ways of man did crumble from these good times.

For many had lived by cruelty and with deceit; and GOD saw that the wickedness of man was great in the earth, and that every imagination of the thoughts of his heart was only evil continually. And it repented the LORD that he had made man on the earth, and it grieved him at his heart. And the LORD said, I will destroy man whom I have created from the face of the earth; both man, and beast, and the creeping thing, and the fowls of the air; for it repenteth me that I have made them. But Noah found grace in the eyes of the LORD.

Noah is Instructed
to Build an Ark

hese are the generations of Noah: Noah was a just man and perfect in his generations, and Noah walked with God and wifed Emzara. And Emzara sat upon the thighs of Noah at once; and she was filled with gladness. And in other years, she lay below him; and Noah was above and their secrets, and their goodness came unto one. And in later years still did Noah lay behind Emzara, and taste of her ear as he knew her. Emzara and Noah sat upon the garden in the day, and in the night. And the moon was a friend to the womb of Emzara; and the sun was a friend to the seed of Noah. And Noah begat three sons, Shem, Ham, and Japheth. The earth also was corrupt before God, and the earth was filled with violence. And God looked upon the earth, and, behold, it was corrupt; for all flesh had forgotten to gift flesh with kindness, and with love; and hence corrupted his way upon the earth. And God said unto Noah, The end of all flesh is come before me; for the earth is filled with violence through them; and, behold, I will destroy them with the earth.

Make thee an ark of gopher wood; rooms shalt thou make in the ark, and shalt pitch it within and without with pitch. And this is the fashion which thou shalt make it of: The length of the ark shall be three hundred cubits, the breadth of it fifty cubits, and the height of it thirty cubits. A window shalt thou make to the ark, and in a cubit shalt thou finish it above; and the door of the ark shalt thou set in the side thereof; with lower, second, and third stories shalt thou make it. And, behold, I, even I, do bring a flood of waters upon the earth, to destroy all flesh, wherein is the breath of life, from under heaven; and every thing that is in the earth shall die. But with thee will I establish my covenant; and thou shalt come into the ark, thou, and thy sons, and thy wife, and thy sons' wives with thee. And of every living thing of all flesh, two of every sort shalt thou bring into the ark, to keep them alive with thee; they shall be male and female. Of fowls after their kind, and of cattle after their kind, of every creeping thing of the earth after his kind, two of every sort shall come unto thee, to keep them alive. And take thou unto thee of all food that is eaten, and thou shalt gather it to thee; and it shall be for food for thee, and for them. Thus did Noah; according to all that God commanded him, so did he.

And the LORD said unto Noah, Come thou and all thy house into the ark; for thee have I seen righteous before me in this generation and the ways that thou rememberest the garden in its blessedness. Of every clean beast thou shalt take to thee by sevens, the male and his female: and of beasts that are not clean by two, the male and his female. Of fowls also of the air by sevens, the male and the female; to keep seed alive upon the face of all the earth. For yet seven days, and I will cause it to rain upon the earth forty days and forty nights; and every living substance that I have made will I destroy from off the face of the earth. And Noah did according unto all that the LORD commanded him. And Noah was six hundred years old when the flood of waters was upon the earth.

And Noah went in, and his sons, and Emzara his wife, and his sons' wives with him, into the ark, because of the waters of the flood. Of clean beasts, and of beasts that are not clean, and of fowls, and of every thing that creepeth upon the earth, There went in two and two unto Noah into the ark, the male and the female, as God had commanded Noah. And it came to pass after seven days, that the waters of the flood were upon the earth.

In the six hundredth year of Noah's life, in the second month, the seventeenth day of the month, the same day were all the fountains of the great deep broken up, and the windows of heaven were opened. And the rain was upon the earth forty days and forty nights. In the selfsame day entered Noah, and Shem, and Ham, and Japheth, the sons of Noah, and Emzara Noah's wife, and Sedeqetelebab, Naeltamauk, and Adataneses, the three wives of his sons with them, into the ark; They, and every beast after his kind, and all the cattle after their kind, and every creeping thing that creepeth upon the earth after his kind, and every fowl after his kind, every bird of every sort. And they went in unto Noah into the ark, two and two of all flesh, wherein is the breath of life. And they that went in, went in male and female of all flesh, as God had commanded him: and the LORD shut him in. Noah and Emzara his wife had a room pitched with pitch within and without. So did the same for Shem, Ham, and Japheth. And from within that pitched room, they did fear what was to come. And they held upon each other for comforts in their trembling.

The Great Flood

nd the flood was forty days upon the earth; and the waters increased, and bare up the ark, and it was lift up above the earth. And the waters prevailed, and were increased greatly upon the earth; and the ark went upon the face of the waters. And the waters prevailed exceedingly upon the earth; and all the high hills, that were under the whole heaven, were covered. Fifteen cubits upward did the waters prevail; and the mountains were covered.

And as the mountains were covered by the waters, so the wives did cover their husband; and the husbands were covered by their wives. In fear they did retreat to the heat of their thighs, so that they might live upon the ark. Emzara did entreat Noah to haven in her breast; and he did haven there. Sedeqetelebab did pray for strength in the staff of Shem; and she did find her heart there. Naeltamauk did find her might in her mouth; and Ham did worship the LORD there. Adataneses and Japheth did creep in the night; and they did eat of each other's secrets to rise up against their fears. And in finding the fruit of the garden every day did God bless them those who were to survive the terrible flood.

And the flood did not abate. And all flesh died that moved upon the earth, both of fowl, and of cattle, and of beast, and of every creeping thing that creepeth upon the earth, and every man and every woman: All in whose nostrils was the breath of life, of all that was in the dry land, died. And every living substance was destroyed which was upon the face of the ground, both man, and cattle, and the creeping things, and the fowl of the heaven; and they were destroyed from the earth: and Noah only remained alive, and they that were with him in the ark. And the waters prevailed upon the earth an hundred and fifty days. But as all perished, Noah, Shem, Ham, Japheth, and their wives yet lived; for they found their way to the garden. Turned they did to each other in grateful embrace, and not the violence that was hated by God.

And God remembered Noah, and every living thing, and all the cattle that was with him in the ark: and God made a wind to pass over the earth, and the waters asswaged; The fountains also of the deep and the windows of heaven were stopped, and the rain from heaven was restrained; And the waters returned from off the earth continually: and after the end of the hundred and fifty days the waters were abated. And the ark rested in the seventh month, on the seventeenth day of the month, upon the mountains of Ararat. And the waters decreased continually until the tenth month: in the tenth month, on the first day of the month, were the tops of the mountains seen.

And it came to pass at the end of forty days, that Noah opened the window of the ark which he had made: And he sent forth a raven, which went forth to and fro, until the waters were dried up from off the earth. But the waters flowed gently from the four rivers upon the ark. And the rivers upon the ark were named Emzara, Sedeqetelebab, Naeltamauk, and Adataneses. And the husbands made prayers in gratitude for the waters of the rivers, and bathed, and drank in the shallows; for the day of freedom was to come. Also Noah sent forth a dove from him, to see if the waters were abated from off the face of the ground; But the dove found no rest for the sole of her foot, and she returned unto him into the ark, for the waters were on the face of the whole earth: then he put forth his hand, and took her, and pulled her in unto him into the ark. And he stayed yet other seven days; and again he sent forth the dove out of the ark; And the dove came in to him in the evening; and, lo, in her mouth was an olive leaf pluckt off: so Noah knew that the waters were abated from off the earth. And he stayed yet other seven days; and sent forth the dove; which returned not again unto him any more.

And it came to pass in the six hundredth and first year, in the first month, the first day of the month, the waters were dried up from off the earth: and Noah removed the covering of the ark, and looked, and, behold, the face of the ground was dry. And in the second month, on the seven and twentieth day of the month, was the earth dried.

Noah Leaves the Ark

And God spake unto Noah, saying, Go forth of the ark, thou, and thy wife, and thy sons, and thy sons' wives with thee. Bring forth with thee every living thing that is with thee, of all flesh, both of fowl, and of cattle, and of every creeping thing that creepeth upon the earth; that they may breed abundantly in the earth, and be fruitful, and multiply upon the earth. And Noah went forth, and his sons, and his wife, and his sons' wives with him: Every beast, every creeping thing, and every fowl, and whatsoever creepeth upon the earth, after their kinds, went forth out of the ark.

And Noah builded an altar unto the LORD; and took of every clean beast, and of every clean fowl, and offered burnt offerings on the altar. And the LORD smelled a sweet savour; and the LORD said in his heart, I will not again curse the ground any more for man's sake; for the imagination of man's heart is evil from his youth; neither will I again smite any more every thing living, as I have done. While the earth remaineth, seedtime and harvest, and cold and heat, and summer and winter, and day and night shall not cease. And Naeltamauk made oils of the fat of the clean beasts, and spiced it with scents pleasing to man, and woman, and the

LORD. And she shared the oil; and she spread it upon her breast, and upon her secrets, and upon the secrets of her secrets. The oil was shared unto the hands of Sedeqetelebab, Adataneses, and Emzara who spread the oil upon their backs and thighs. And by their staffs and by their hands did their husbands move upon their secrets and the secrets of their secrets. Then the wives tasted all of spices and oils; and the husbands rejoiced in the thighs of their wives, and plowed upon the fertile ground. For the LORD hath delivered them from floods, and given them joy in the scented garden.

And God blessed Noah and his sons, and said unto them, Be fruitful, and multiply, and replenish the earth. And the fear of you and the dread of you shall be upon every beast of the earth, and upon every fowl of the air, upon all that moveth upon the earth, and upon all the fishes of the sea; into your hand are they delivered. Every moving thing that liveth shall be meat for you; even as the green herb have I given you all things. But flesh with the life thereof, which is the blood thereof, shall ye not eat. And surely your blood of your lives will I require; at the hand of every beast will I require it, and at the hand of man; at the hand of every man's brother will I require the life of man. Whoso sheddeth man's blood, by man shall his blood be shed: for in the image of God made he man. And you, be ye fruitful, and multiply; bring forth abundantly in the earth, and multiply therein.

And God spake unto Noah, and to his sons with him, saying, And I, behold, I establish my covenant with you, and with your seed after you; And with every living creature that is with you, of the fowl, of the cattle, and of every beast of the earth with you; from all that go out of the ark, to every beast of the earth. And I will establish my covenant with you; neither shall all flesh be cut off any more by the waters of a flood; neither shall there any more be a flood to destroy the earth. And God said, This is the token of the covenant which I make between me and you and every living creature that is with you, for perpetual generations: I do set my bow in the cloud, and it shall be for a token of a covenant between me and the earth. And it shall come to pass, when I bring a cloud over the earth, that the bow shall be seen in the cloud: And I will remember my covenant, which is between me and you and every living creature of all flesh; and the waters shall no more become a flood to destroy all flesh. And the bow shall be in the cloud; and I will look upon it, that I may remember the everlasting covenant between God and every living creature of all flesh that is upon the earth. And God said unto Noah, This is the token of the covenant, which I have established between me and all flesh that is upon the earth.

And the sons of Noah, that went forth of the ark, were Shem, and Ham, and Japheth: and Ham is the father of Canaan. These are the three sons of Noah: and of them was the whole earth overspread. And Noah began to be an husbandman, and he planted a vineyard: And he drank of the wine, and was drunken; and he was uncovered within his tent. And Ham, the father of Canaan, saw the nakedness of his father, and told his two brethren without. And Shem and Japheth took a garment, and laid it upon both their shoulders, and went backward, and covered the nakedness of their father; and their faces were backward, and they saw not their father's nakedness. And Noah awoke from his wine, and knew what his younger son had done unto him. And he said, Cursed be Canaan; a servant of servants shall he be unto his brethren. And he said, Blessed be the LORD God of Shem; and Canaan shall be his servant. God shall enlarge Japheth, and he shall dwell in the tents of Shem; and Canaan shall be his servant.

And Noah lived after the flood three hundred and fifty years. And all the days of Noah were nine hundred and fifty years: and he died.

The Descendants of Noah

ow these are the generations of the sons of Noah, Shem, Ham, and Japheth: and unto them were sons born after the flood. The sons of Japheth; Gomer, and Magog, and Madai, and Javan, and Tubal, and Meshech, and Tiras. And the sons of Gomer; Ashkenaz, and Riphath, and Togarmah. And the sons of Javan; Elishah, and Tarshish, Kittim, and Dodanim. By these were the isles of the Gentiles divided in their lands; every one after his tongue, after their families, in their nations.

And the sons of Ham; Cush, and Mizraim, and Phut, and Canaan. And the sons of Cush; Seba, and Havilah, and Sabtah, and Raamah, and Sabtechah: and the sons of Raamah; Sheba, and Dedan.

And Cush begat Nimrod: he began to be a mighty one in the earth. He was a mighty hunter before the LORD: wherefore it is said, Even as Nimrod the mighty hunter before the LORD. And the beginning of his kingdom was Babel, and Erech, and Accad, and Calneh, in the land of Shinar. Out of that land went forth Asshur, and builded Nineveh, and the city Rehoboth, and Calah, And Resen between Nineveh and Calah: the same is a great city.

And Mizraim begat Ludim, and Anamim, and Lehabim, and Naphtuhim, And Pathrusim, and Casluhim, (out of whom came Philistim,) and Caphtorim.

And Canaan begat Sidon his firstborn, and Heth, And the Jebusite, and the Amorite, and the Girgasite, And the Hivite, and the Arkite, and the Sinite, And the Arvadite, and the Zemarite, and the Hamathite: and afterward were the families of the Canaanites spread abroad. And the border of the Canaanites was from Sidon, as thou comest to Gerar, unto Gaza; as thou goest, unto Sodom, and Gomorrah, and Admah, and Zeboim, even unto Lasha. These are the sons of Ham, after their families, after their tongues, in their countries, and in their nations.

Unto Shem also, the father of all the children of Eber, the brother of Japheth the elder, even to him were children born. The children of Shem; Elam, and Asshur, and Arphaxad, and Lud, and Aram. And the children of Aram; Uz, and Hul, and Gether, and Mash. And Arphaxad begat Salah; and Salah begat Eber.

And unto Eber were born two sons: the name of one was Peleg; for in his days was the earth divided; and his brother's name was Joktan. And Joktan begat Almodad, and Sheleph, and Hazarmaveth, and Jerah, And Hadoram, and Uzal, and Diklah, And Obal, and Abimael, and Sheba, And Ophir, and Havilah, and Jobab: all these were the sons of Joktan. And their dwelling was from Mesha, as thou goest unto Sephar a mount of the east. These are the sons of Shem, after their families, after their tongues, in their lands, after their nations. These are the families of the sons of Noah, after their generations, in their nations: and by these were the nations divided in the earth after the flood.

The Tower of Babel

nd the whole earth was of one language, and of one speech. And it came to pass, as they journeyed from the east, that they found a plain in the land of Shinar; and they dwelt there. And they said one to another, Go to, let us make brick, and burn them thoroughly. And they had brick for stone, and slime had they for morter. And they said, Go to, let us build us a city and a tower, whose top may reach unto heaven; and let us make us a name, lest we be scattered abroad upon the face of the whole earth. And the LORD came down to see the city and the tower, which the children of men builded. And the LORD said, Behold, the people is one, and they have all one language; and this they begin to do: and now nothing will be restrained from them, which they have imagined to do. Go to, let us go down, and there confound their language, that they may not understand one another's speech. So the LORD scattered them abroad from thence upon the face of all the earth: and they left off to build the city. Therefore is the name of it called Babel; because the LORD did there confound the language of all the earth: and from thence did the LORD scatter them abroad upon the face of all the earth. And, lo, this was the mark on the people, as Cain had been marked before. And this mark, set upon them of the confounded languages, did not keep the people from their desire to build. And they did find that the mark made unto them all secrets. And they did want to know the secrets. For secrets pray only to be discovered, and known. And the sounds of new tongues did lap along hearts and stir thighs.

These are the generations of Shem: Shem was an hundred years old, and begat Arphaxad two years after the flood: And Shem lived after he begat Arphaxad five hundred years, and begat sons and daughters.

And Arphaxad lived five and thirty years, and begat Salah: And Arphaxad lived after he begat Salah four hundred and three years, and begat sons and daughters.

And Salah lived thirty years, and begat Eber: And Salah lived after he begat Eber four hundred and three years, and begat sons and daughters.

And Eber lived four and thirty years, and begat Peleg: And Eber lived after he begat Peleg four hundred and thirty years, and begat sons and daughters. And Peleg lived thirty years, and begat Reu:

And Peleg lived after he begat Reu two hundred and nine years, and begat sons and daughters.

And Reu lived two and thirty years, and begat Serug: And Reu lived after he begat Serug two hundred and seven years, and begat sons and daughters. And Serug lived thirty years, and begat Nahor:

And Serug lived after he begat Nahor two hundred years, and begat sons and daughters.

And Nahor lived nine and twenty years, and begat Terah:

And Nahor lived after he begat Terah an hundred and nineteen years, and begat sons and daughters. And Terah lived seventy years, and begat Abram, Nahor, and Haran.

Terah's Descendants

Now these are the generations of Terah: Terah begat Abram, Nahor, and Haran; and Haran begat Lot. And Haran died before his father Terah in the land of his nativity, in Ur of the Chaldees. And Abram and Nahor took them wives: the name of Abram's wife was Sarai; and the name of Nahor's wife, Milcah, the daughter of Haran, the father of Milcah, and the father of Iscah. But Sarai was barren; she had no child. Abram and Sarai knew of each other's secrets, and of each other's secrets they knew. They pressed thighs in hope for a child. But there was none. And close to each others embraces were kept, as they lay naked, with the sun and the moon, day and night they turned, like loving serpents in hope of a child. In the days, they looked for the garden but found it not. But in the nights, they did find and rest in the garden; but yet there was no child.

And Terah took Abram his son, and Lot the son of Haran his son's son, and Sarai his daughter in law, his son Abram's wife; and they went forth with them from Ur of the Chaldees, to go into the land of Canaan; and they came unto Haran, and dwelt there. And the days of Terah were two hundred and five years: and Terah died in Haran.

The Call of Abram

ow the LORD had said unto Abram, Get thee out of thy country, and from thy kindred, and from thy father's house, unto a land that I will shew thee: And I will make of thee a great nation, and I will bless thee, and make thy name great; and thou shalt be a blessing: And I will bless them that bless thee, and curse him that curseth thee: and in thee shall all families of the earth be blessed. So Abram departed, as the LORD had spoken unto him; and Lot went with him: and Abram was seventy and five years old when he departed out of Haran. And Abram took Sarai his wife, and Lot his brother's son, and all their substance that they had gathered, and the souls that they had gotten in Haran; and they went forth to go into the land of Canaan; and into the land of Canaan they came.

And Abram passed through the land unto the place of Sichem, unto the plain of Moreh. And the Canaanite was then in the land. And the LORD appeared unto Abram, and said, Unto thy seed will I give this land: and there builded he an altar unto the LORD, who appeared unto him. And he removed from thence unto a mountain on the east of Bethel, and pitched his tent, having Bethel on the west, and Hai on the east: and there he builded an altar unto the LORD, and called upon the name of the LORD. And Abram journeyed, going on still toward the south.

Abram Sojourns to Egypt

nd there was a famine in the land: and Abram went down into Egypt to sojourn there; for the famine was grievous in the land. And it came to pass, when he was come near to enter into Egypt, that he said unto Sarai his wife, Behold now, I know that thou art a fair woman to look upon in thy skins, with the ochre within thine eyes. The joints of thy hips move with love for the LORD, and for his creation. Therefore it shall come to pass, when the Egyptians shall see thee, that they shall say, This is his wife: and they will kill me, but they will save thee alive. Say, I pray thee, thou art my sister: that it may be well with me for thy sake; and my soul shall live, because of thee. For I crave for my soul to live so that I might be with thee joint to joint.

And it came to pass, that, when Abram was come into Egypt, the Egyptians beheld the woman that she was very fair. The princes also of Pharaoh saw her, and commended her before Pharaoh: and the woman was taken into Pharaoh's house. And Sarai kept Abram safe by her hand. The Pharaoh craved to know the secrets under the skins of Sarai, and to see her beg for the pleasures of her thighs. And the ochre in her eyes enflamed Pharaoh. And Pharaoh did use his crook upon her. And Sarai ventured to show her fervour when she clasped the Pharaoh. And with flail and crook did they know each other unto the day. And the welts upon their backs and thighs were cooled by kisses; and kisses did cool the welts. Sarai bit upon his crook with ardour; and he brought seed from within Sarai, and watered it. And Abram did keep watch, and abide by them in the night. His staff stood in secret for Sarai.

And so Pharaoh entreated Abram well for her sake: and he had sheep, and oxen, and he asses, and menservants, and maidservants, and she asses, and camels. And the LORD plagued Pharaoh and his house with great plagues because of Sarai Abram's wife. And Pharaoh called Abram, and said, What is this that thou hast done unto me? Why didst thou not tell me that she was thy wife? Why saidst thou, She is my sister? so I might have taken her to me to wife: now therefore behold thy wife, take her, and go thy way. And Pharaoh commanded his men concerning him: and they sent him away, and his wife, and all that he had. And Pharaoh took a maiden whom he begat by his concubines called Hagar , and he gave her to Sarai for a handmaid.

And Abram went up out of Egypt, he, and his wife Sarai, and all that he had, and Lot with him, into the south. And Abram was very rich in cattle, in silver, and in gold. And he went on his journeys from the south even to Bethel, unto the place where his tent had been at the beginning, between Bethel and Hai; Unto the place of the altar, which he had made there at the first: and there Abram called on the name of the LORD.

And Lot also, which went with Abram, had flocks, and herds, and tents. And the land was not able to bear them, that they might dwell together: for their substance was great, so that they could not dwell together. And there was a strife between the herdmen of Abram's cattle and the herdmen of

Lot's cattle: and the Canaanite and the Perizzite dwelled then in the land. And Abram said unto Lot, Let there be no strife, I pray thee, between me and thee, and between my herdmen and thy herdmen; for we be brethren. Is not the whole land before thee? Separate thyself, I pray thee, from me: if thou wilt take the left hand, then I will go to the right; or if thou depart to the right hand, then I will go to the left. And Lot lifted up his eyes, and beheld all the plain of Jordan, that it was well watered every where, before the LORD destroyed Sodom and Gomorrah, even as the garden of the LORD, like the land of Egypt, as thou comest unto Zoar. Then Lot chose him all the plain of Jordan; and Lot journeyed east: and they separated themselves the one from the other. Abram dwelled in the land of Canaan, and Lot dwelled in the cities of the plain, and pitched his tent toward Sodom. But the men of Sodom were wicked and sinners before the LORD exceedingly.

And the LORD said unto Abram, after that Lot was separated from him, Lift up now thine eyes, and look from the place where thou art northward, and southward, and eastward, and westward: For all the land which thou seest, to thee will I give it, and to thy seed for ever. And I will make thy seed as the dust of the earth: so that if a man can number the dust of the earth, then shall thy seed also be numbered. Arise, walk through the land in the length of it and in the breadth of it; for I will give it unto thee. Then Abram removed his tent, and came and dwelt in the plain of Mamre, which is in Hebron, and built there an altar unto the LORD.

War With the Kings
From the East

And it came to pass in the days of Amraphel king of Shinar, Arioch king of Ellasar, Chedorlaomer king of Elam, and Tidal king of nations; That these made war with Bera king of Sodom, and with Birsha king of Gomorrah, Shinab king of Admah, and Shemeber king of Zeboiim, and the king of Bela, which is Zoar. All these were joined together in the vale of Siddim, which is the salt sea. Twelve years they served Chedorlaomer, and in the thirteenth year they rebelled. And in the fourteenth year came Chedorlaomer, and the kings that were with him, and smote the Rephaims in Ashteroth Karnaim, and the Zuzims in Ham, and the Emims in Shaveh Kiriathaim, And the Horites in their mount Seir, unto El-paran, which is by the wilderness. And they returned, and came to En-mishpat, which is Kadesh, and smote all the country of the Amalekites, and also the Amorites that dwelt in Hazezon-tamar. And there went out the king of Sodom, and the king of Gomorrah, and the king of Admah, and the king of Zeboiim, and the king of Bela (the same is Zoar;) and they joined battle with them in the vale of Siddim; With Chedorlaomer the king of Elam, and with Tidal king of nations, and Amraphel king of Shinar, and Arioch king of Ellasar; four kings with five. And the vale of Siddim was full of slimepits; and the kings of Sodom and Gomorrah fled, and fell there; and they that remained fled to the mountain. And they took all the goods of Sodom and Gomorrah, and all their victuals, and went their way. And they took Lot, Abram's brother's son, who dwelt in Sodom, and his goods, and departed.

And Amraphel king of Shinar, Arioch king of Ellasar, Chedorlaomer king of Elam, and Tidal king of nations took Lot to a tent high above the vale of Siddim. And there they spoke to Lot, Why didst thou this thing against us? The good that we have done for thee is great. And now we have spent treasure and spilled blood all along the vale of Siddim to quell thee as rebel when once we were but friends. We have presently been far from from our homes now more than one year, and are covered in filth and slime. And yet we have spared thee from death.

And Lot said unto the prevailing kings, lo, no claim couldest be made unto thy throne now. Let me bless, and prize thee as good hosts. Let me kneel at thy feet, and wash them. Open thy mouths; and I shall feed thee with fruits, and with meats, and with bread. Turn thy head to me; and I shall tend to thy brow; and lie prone; and I shall oil thy backs. And Lot did kneel at the feet of Amraphel, Arioch, Chedorlaomer, and Tidal; and he did bathe them, and washed them of their filth and their slime. And the heels of the kings were made clean with waters, and made smooth by the hands of Lot. And the kings were fed and their backs were oiled. And the staffs of the kings stood in the night, as Lot shared of the milk of the kings with the kings.

And there came one that had escaped, and told Abram the Hebrew; for he dwelt in the plain of Mamre the Amorite, brother of Eshcol, and brother of Aner: and these were confederate with Abram. And when Abram heard that his brother was taken captive, he armed his trained servants, born in his own house, three hundred and eighteen, and pursued them unto Dan. And he divided himself against them, he and his servants, by night, and smote them, and pursued them unto Hobah, which is on the left hand of Damascus. And he brought back all the goods, and also brought again his brother Lot, and his goods, and the women also, and the people. And Abram did taste of every woman, so that his seed might number the stars, and fill the land in its length and breadth. But no seed came with his tastings.

And the king of Sodom went out to meet him after his return from the slaughter of Chedorlaomer, and of the kings that were with him, at the valley of Shaveh, which is the king's dale. And Melchizedek king of Salem brought forth bread and wine: and he was the priest of the most high God. And he blessed him, and said, Blessed be Abram of the most high God, possessor of heaven and earth: And blessed be the most high God, which hath delivered thine enemies into thy hand. And he gave him tithes of all. And the king of Sodom said unto Abram, Give me the persons, and take the goods to thyself. And Abram said to the king of Sodom, I have lift up mine hand unto the LORD, the most high God, the possessor of heaven and earth, That I will not take from a thread even to a shoelatchet, and that I will not take any thing that is thine, lest thou shouldest say, I have made Abram rich: Save only that which the young men have eaten, and the portion of the men which went with me, Aner, Eshcol, and Mamre; let them take their portion.

After these things the word of the LORD came unto Abram in a vision, saying, Fear not, Abram: I am thy shield, and thy exceeding great reward. And Abram said, Lord GOD, what wilt thou give me, seeing I go childless, and the steward of my house is this Eliezer of Damascus? And Abram said, Behold, to me thou hast given no seed: and, lo, one born in my house is mine heir. And, behold, the word of the LORD came unto him, saying, This shall not be thine heir; but he that shall come forth out of thine own bowels shall be thine heir. And he brought him forth abroad, and said, Look now toward heaven, and tell the stars, if thou be able to number them: and he said unto him, So shall thy seed be. And he believed in the LORD; and he counted it to him for righteousness. And he said unto him, I am the LORD that brought thee out of Ur of the Chaldees, to give thee this land to inherit it. And he said, Lord GOD, whereby shall I know that I shall inherit it? And he said unto him, Take me an heifer of three years old, and a she goat of three years old, and a ram of three years old, and a turtledove, and a young pigeon. And he took unto him all these, and divided them in the midst, and laid each piece one against another: but the birds divided he not. And when the fowls came down upon the carcases, Abram drove them away.

And when the sun was going down, a deep sleep fell upon Abram; and, lo, a horror of great darkness fell upon him. And he said unto Abram, Know of a surety that thy seed shall be a stranger in a land that is not theirs, and shall serve them; and they shall afflict them four hundred years; And also that nation, whom they shall serve, will I judge: and afterward shall they come out with great substance. And thou shalt go to thy fathers in peace; thou shalt be buried in a good old age. But in the fourth generation they shall come hither again: for the iniquity of the Amorites is not yet full. And it came to pass, that, when the sun went down, and it was dark, behold a smoking furnace, and a burning lamp that passed between those pieces. In the same day the LORD made a covenant with Abram, saying, Unto thy seed have I given this land, from the river of Egypt unto the great river, the river Euphrates: The Kenites, and the Kenizzites, and the Kadmonites, And the Hittites, and the Perizzites, and the Rephaims, And the Amorites, and the Canaanites, and the Girgashites, and the Jebusites.

The Birth of Ishmael

ow Sarai Abram's wife bare him no children: and she had an handmaid, an Egyptian, whose name was Hagar. And Sarai said unto Abram, Behold now, the LORD hath restrained me from bearing: I pray thee, go in unto my maid; it may be that I may obtain children by her. And Sarai spake unto Hagar, and said, Ye shall cleve unto Abram, and taste of him; but you may not eat from every tree of the garden of Abram. But the oil of the tree which is in the midst of the garden, Ye shall not eat of it, neither shall ye touch it by thy hand, lest ye forget my wroth.

And Abram hearkened to the voice of Sarai. And Sàrai Abram's wife took Hagar her maid the Egyptian, after Abram had dwelt ten years in the land of Canaan, and gave her to her husband Abram to be his wife. And Sarai sent Hagar to Abram with gladness, and spied upon their tent as Abram knew Hagar.

And Abram went in unto Hagar, and ate of her fruit. Abram rejoiced with glad tidings in the breasts of Hagar; for he had longed for her newness. And Hagar in her newness hungered for Abram like a calf for milk. The secret ways of the Egyptians were known by Hagar; and her thighs did tell of those secrets. And as she spied upon the secrets that Hagar knew in the dark tent, the waters of Sarai gently ran; and her breast was of fire. But the secrets vexed her; and she craved to know, and to see them clearly. And Abram anointed his pillar, so that it might support the temple of Hagar. And his pillar did bow at the jewel at the temple gate; and his oil did spill. And Hagar tasted of his oil, but kept the sacrifice for her self; and Hagar was full of hope. And, lo, she conceived. And when Hagar saw that she had conceived, her mistress was despised in her eyes; for Hagar wanted Abram for herself alone. And Sarai knew this, and said unto Abram, My wrong be upon thee: I have given my maid into thy bosom; and when she saw that she had conceived, I was despised in her eyes: the LORD judge between me and thee; for I only desire to be treasured by thee, and the LORD alone. But Abram said unto Sarai, Behold, thy maid is in thy hand; do to her as it pleaseth thee. And Sarai said to Abram that Hagar the Egyptian had sworn an oath to her, and had forgotten it for she hadst seen Hagar taste what was not to be tasted.

And so Sarai didst claim Abram with her words to Hagar. And Sarai struck Hagar with anger; because Hagar rebelled against her place as an handmaid, and tried to stand as wife to Abram. And she made Hagar reveal the secrets of the Egyptians that she did not understand, and tell of her time with Abram. And Sarai said, Thou hast known that I was happy for thee to know Abram, and to conceive; but now thou hast pushed beyond the gate of welcome; for thou art only a maid. When Sarai dealt hardly with Hagar, she fled from her face.

And the angel of the LORD found Hagar, Sarai's maid by a fountain of water in the wilderness, by the fountain in the way to Shur. And he said, Hagar, Sarai's maid, whence camest thou? and whither wilt thou go? And she said, I flee from the face of my mistress Sarai. And the angel of the LORD said

unto her, Return to thy mistress, and submit thyself under
her hands. Let Sarai set her hands upon the jewel that sits
at the gate of your temple, where Abram did worship. And
the angel of the LORD said unto her, I will multiply thy seed
exceedingly, that it shall not be numbered for multitude. And
the angel of the LORD said unto her, Behold, thou art with
child, and shalt bear a son, and shalt call his name Ishmael;
because the LORD hath heard thy affliction. And he will be
a wild man; his hand will be against every man, and every
man's hand against him; and he shall dwell in the presence
of all his brethren. And she called the name of the LORD
that spake unto her, Thou God seest me: for she said, Have
I also here looked after him that seeth me? Wherefore the
well was called Beer-lahai-roi; behold, it is between Kadesh
and Bered.

And Hagar bare Abram a son: and Abram called his son's
name, which Hagar bare, Ishmael. And Abram was fourscore
and six years old, when Hagar bare Ishmael to Abram.

The Covenant with Abraham

nd when Abram was ninety years old and nine, the LORD appeared to Abram, and said unto him, I am the Almighty God; walk before me, and be thou perfect. And I will make my covenant between me and thee, and will multiply thee exceedingly. And Abram fell on his face: and God talked with him, saying, As for me, behold, my covenant is with thee, and thou shalt be a father of many nations. Neither shall thy name any more be called Abram, but thy name shall be Abraham; for a father of many nations have I made thee. And I will make thee exceeding fruitful, and I will make nations of thee, and kings shall come out of thee. And I will establish my covenant between me and thee and thy seed after thee in their generations for an everlasting covenant, to be a God unto thee, and to thy seed after thee. And I will give unto thee, and to thy seed after thee, the land wherein thou art a stranger, all the land of Canaan, for an everlasting possession; and I will be their God.

And God said unto Abraham, Thou shalt keep my covenant therefore, thou, and thy seed after thee in their generations. This is my covenant, which ye shall keep, between me and you and thy seed after thee; Every man child among you shall be circumcised. And ye shall circumcise the flesh of your foreskin; and it shall be a token of the covenant betwixt me and you. And he that is eight days old shall be circumcised among you, every man child in your generations, he that is born in the house, or bought with money of any stranger, which is not of thy seed. He that is born in thy house, and he that is bought with thy money, must needs be circumcised: and my covenant shall be in your flesh for an everlasting covenant. And the uncircumcised man child whose flesh of his foreskin is not circumcised, that soul shall be cut off from his people; he hath broken my covenant. For the gate must be open; and the path must be clear, so that the blessing of the LORD shall arrive unto men. But his blessings will be summoned unto all women; for the LORD resides in the deepest hearts of women, and his blessing will be risen unto them.

And God said unto Abraham, As for Sarai thy wife, thou shalt not call her name Sarai, but Sarah shall her name be. And I will bless her, and give thee a son also of her: yea, I will bless her, and she shall be a mother of nations; kings of people shall be of her. Then Abraham fell upon his face, and laughed, and said in his heart, Shall a child be born unto him that is an hundred years old? and shall Sarah, that is ninety years old, bear? And Abraham said unto God, O that Ishmael might live before thee! And God said, Sarah thy wife shall bear thee a son indeed; and thou shalt call his name Isaac: and I will establish my covenant with him for an everlasting covenant, and with his seed after him. And as for Ishmael, I have heard thee: Behold, I have blessed him, and will make him fruitful, and will multiply him exceedingly; twelve princes shall he beget, and I will make him a great nation. But my covenant will I establish with Isaac, which Sarah shall bear unto thee at this set time in the next year. And he left off talking with him, and God went up from Abraham.

And Abraham took Ishmael his son, and all that were born in his house, and all that were bought with his money, every male among the men of Abraham's house; and circumcised the flesh of their foreskin in the selfsame day, as God had said unto him. And Abraham was ninety years old and nine, when he was circumcised in the flesh of his foreskin. And Ishmael his son was thirteen years old, when he was circumcised in the flesh of his foreskin. In the selfsame day was Abraham circumcised, and Ishmael his son. And all the men of his house, born in the house, and bought with money of the stranger, were circumcised with him. And the gate did open; and the path did clear as the LORD blessed them all with his covenant, through the tender flesh of the foreskin. And they didst know of the blessing.

Abraham is Promised a Son

And the LORD appeared unto him in the plains of Mamre: and he sat in the tent door in the heat of the day; And he lift up his eyes and looked, and, lo, three men stood by him: and when he saw them, he ran to meet them from the tent door, and bowed himself toward the ground, And said, My Lord, if now I have found favour in thy sight, pass not away, I pray thee, from thy servant: Let a little water, I pray you, be fetched, and wash your feet, and rest yourselves under the tree: And I will fetch a morsel of bread, and comfort ye your hearts; after that ye shall pass on: for therefore are ye come to your servant. And they said, So do, as thou hast said. And Abraham hastened into the tent unto Sarah and kissed upon her breast and back for gladness; and she did kiss back, and he said, Make ready quickly three measures of fine meal, knead it, and make cakes upon the hearth. And Abraham ran unto the herd, and fetcht a calf tender and good, and gave it unto a young man; and he hasted to dress it. And he took butter, and milk, and the calf which he had dressed, and set it before them; and he stood by them under the tree, and they did eat.

And they said unto him, Where is Sarah thy wife? And he said, Behold, in the tent. And they gave thanks to Abraham for the butter, and milk; but now called Abraham to stay

with them for a day, so that they might rest and bear glad
tidings. And wise Abraham knew them. And he did tend
to their aching thighs with his hands, and from whence his
words came. And he did make them sweet with honey; and
he did make them smooth with milk, and with butter, and
with cream. And they loved the wise host Abraham for that
day. And in gratitude for the sated thighs that Abraham had
made, one of them turned to Abraham and he said, I will
certainly return unto thee according to the time of life; and,
lo, Sarah thy wife shall have a son. And Sarah heard it in
the tent door, which was behind him. Now Abraham and
Sarah were old and well stricken in age; and it ceased to be
with Sarah after the manner of women. Therefore Sarah
laughed within herself, saying, After I am waxed old shall I
have pleasure, my lord being old also? And the LORD said
unto Abraham, Wherefore did Sarah laugh, saying, Shall
I of a surety bear a child, which am old? Is any thing too
hard for the LORD? At the time appointed I will return unto
thee, according to the time of life, and Sarah shall have a
son. Then Sarah denied, saying, I laughed not; for she was
afraid. And he said, Nay; but thou didst laugh. Still the eyes
of Sarah glistered, and her hips still swayed.

Abraham Intercedes for Sodom

And the men rose up from thence, and looked toward Sodom: and Abraham went with them to bring them on the way. And the LORD said, Shall I hide from Abraham that thing which I do; Seeing that Abraham shall surely become a great and mighty nation, and all the nations of the earth shall be blessed in him? For I know him, that he will command his children and his household after him, and they shall keep the way of the LORD, to do justice and judgment; that the LORD may bring upon Abraham that which he hath spoken of him. And the LORD said, Because the cry of Sodom and Gomorrah is great, and because their sin is very grievous; I will go down now, and see whether they have done altogether according to the cry of it, which is come unto me; and if not, I will know.

And the men turned their faces from thence, and went toward Sodom: but Abraham stood yet before the LORD. And Abraham drew near, and said, Wilt thou also destroy the righteous with the wicked? Peradventure there be fifty righteous within the city: wilt thou also destroy and not spare the place for the fifty righteous that are therein? That be far from thee to do after this manner, to slay the righteous with the wicked: and that the righteous should be as the wicked, that be far from thee: Shall not the Judge of all the earth do right? And the LORD said, If I find in Sodom fifty righteous within the city, then I will spare all the place for their sakes. And Abraham answered and said, Behold now, I have taken upon me to speak unto the Lord, which am but dust and ashes: Peradventure there shall lack five of the fifty righteous: wilt thou destroy all the city for lack of five? And he said, If I find there forty and five, I will not destroy it. And he spake unto him yet again, and said, Peradventure there shall be forty found there. And he said, I will not do it for forty's sake. And he said unto him, Oh let not the Lord be angry, and I will speak: Peradventure there shall thirty be found there. And he said, I will not do it, if I find thirty there. And he said, Behold now, I have taken upon me to speak unto the Lord: Peradventure there shall be twenty found there. And he said, I will not destroy it for twenty's sake. And he said, Oh let not the Lord be angry, and I will speak yet but this once: Peradventure ten shall be found there. And he said, I will not destroy it for ten's sake. And the LORD went his way, as soon as he had left communing with Abraham: and Abraham returned unto his place.

And there came two angels to Sodom at even; and Lot sat in the gate of Sodom: and Lot seeing them rose up to meet them; and he bowed himself with his face toward the ground; And he said, Behold now, my lords, turn in, I pray you, into your servant's house, and tarry all night, and wash your feet, and ye shall rise up early, and go on your ways. And they said, Nay; but we will abide in the street all night. And he pressed upon them greatly; and they turned in unto him, and entered into his house; and he made them a feast, and did bake unleavened bread, and they did eat, as was the proper custom. And in sweetness did the angels receive the ministrations of Lot. And Lot did hold them, and lean upon them, as the angels entered his secret house. And they did know the garden. And they did savour the taste of honey, and of milk, and of unleavened bread in a knot together.

But before they lay down, the men of the city, even the men of Sodom, compassed the house round, both old and young, all the people from every quarter: And they called unto Lot, and said unto him, Where are the men which came in to thee this night? bring them out unto us, that we may know them. And Lot went out at the door unto them, and shut the door after him, And said, I pray you, brethren, do not so wickedly. If you are not to offer them cakes and bedding and minister to their flesh, as is the olden custom, why would you press upon them? Behold now, I have two daughters which have not known man; let me, I pray you, bring them out unto you, and do ye to them as is good in your eyes: only unto these men do nothing; for therefore came they under the shadow of my roof. And they said, Stand back. And they said again, This one fellow came in to sojourn, and he will needs be a judge: now will we deal worse with thee, than with them. And they pressed sore upon the man, even Lot, and came near to break the door. But the men put forth their hand, and pulled Lot into the house to them, and shut to the door. And they smote the men that were at the door of the house with blindness, both small and great: so that they wearied themselves to find the door.

And the men said unto Lot, Hast thou here any besides? son in law, and thy sons, and thy daughters, and whatsoever thou hast in the city, bring them out of this place: For we will destroy this place, because the cry of them is waxen great before the face of the LORD; and the LORD hath sent us to destroy it; for it has forgotten how to tend to the blessed strangers of the LORD, and to the poor. And Lot went out, and spake unto his sons in law, which married his daughters, and said, Up, get you out of this place; for the LORD will destroy this city. But he seemed as one that mocked unto his sons in law.

And when the morning arose, then the angels hastened Lot, saying, Arise, take thy wife Edo, and thy two daughters Pheiné and Thamma, which are here; lest thou be consumed in the iniquity of the inhospitable city. And while he lingered, the men laid hold upon his hand, and upon the hand of his wife, and upon the hand of his two daughters; the LORD being merciful unto him: and they brought him forth, and set him without the city.

And it came to pass, when they had brought them forth abroad, that he said, Escape for thy life; look not behind thee, neither stay thou in all the plain; escape to the mountain, lest thou be consumed. And Lot said unto them, Oh, not so, my Lord: Behold now, thy servant hath found grace in thy sight, and thou hast magnified thy mercy, which thou hast shewed unto me in saving my life; and I cannot escape to the mountain, lest some evil take me, and I die: Behold now, this city is near to flee unto, and it is a little one: Oh, let me escape thither, (is it not a little one?) and my soul shall live. And he said unto him, See, I have accepted thee concerning this thing also, that I will not overthrow this city, for the which thou hast spoken. Haste thee, escape thither; for I cannot do any thing till thou be come thither. Therefore the name of the city was called Zoar.

Destruction of Sodom and Gomorrah

he sun was risen upon the earth when Lot entered into Zoar. Then the LORD rained upon Sodom and upon Gomorrah brimstone and fire from the LORD out of heaven; And he overthrew those cities, and all the plain, and all the inhabitants of the cities, and that which grew upon the ground.

But his wife Edo looked back from behind him, and she became a pillar of salt.

And Abraham gat up early in the morning to the place where he stood before the LORD: And he looked toward Sodom and Gomorrah, and toward all the land of the plain, and beheld, and, lo, the smoke of the country went up as the smoke of a furnace.

And it came to pass, when God destroyed the cities of the plain, that God remembered Abraham, and sent Lot out of the midst of the overthrow, when he overthrew the cities in the which Lot dwelt.

And Lot went up out of Zoar, and dwelt in the mountain, and his two daughters Pheine and Thamma with him; for he feared to dwell in Zoar: and he dwelt in a cave, he and his two daughters. And the elder Pheiné said unto the younger, Woe betide us all for the LORD hath destroyed the world again for his namesake. For the cities on the plain cared not any longer how to tend to those in most need and poor. And now our father is old, and there is not a man in the earth to come in unto us after the manner of all the earth. For our father is now in great need, and we were once offered as gifts to men to give succour. Come, let us make our father drink wine, and we will lie with him, that we may preserve the seed of our father, and tend to him, and replenish the earth. And they made their father drink wine that night: and the firstborn went in, and lay with her father, while the younger sat at the gate of the tent to watch; and he perceived not fully when she lay athwart him, nor when she arose. And yet in his drink he did rise to meet his firstborn upon her thighs. And she did taste the salt of her father from his breast; and he did fill her with his salt and cured her womb. And Thamma didst feel her hungers rise, and her thighs widen. She longed to fill the world, as her father would fill her.

And it came to pass on the morrow, that Pheiné said unto Thamma, Behold, you gazed upon how I lay yesternight with my father, and how I tended to his needs, and to mine; I spied the hunger in thy breast. Yea, now I am with child and your womb may be filled hence. Let us make him drink wine this night also; and go thou in, and lie with him, that we may preserve seed of our father, and fill the world. And they made their father drink wine that night also: and Thamma arose, and lay with him and he perceived not when she lay down, nor when she arose. She called forth the staff of Lot, and had her flock tended by it. And the wool of her thighs wove with the wool of her father, to make one wool. And Pheine did watch, and did lift her skins to explore the lesser cave within where only one lived. Thus were both the daughters of Lot

with child by their father. And the firstborn Pheine bare a
son, and called his name Moab: the same is the father of the
Moabites unto this day. And the younger Thamma, she also
bare a son, and called his name Benammi: the same is the
father of the children of Ammon unto this day.

Abraham at Gerar

And Abraham journeyed from thence toward the south country, and dwelled between Kadesh and Shur, and sojourned in Gerar. And Abraham said of Sarah his wife, She is my sister: and Abimelech king of Gerar sent, and took Sarah; and she danced for Abimelech, with drummers and veils. And she did flash her ochre eyes with wanting, as she offered her breast and thighs. But long was the day; and Abimelech did set only his eyes upon Sarah. And he raised his staff to her in a count of one, and oiled the floor, and set himself to sleep. But God came to Abimelech in a dream by night, and said to him, Behold, thou art but a dead man, for the woman which thou hast taken; for she is a man's wife. But Abimelech had not come near her; he had only gazed upon her from across the room: and he said, Lord, wilt thou slay also a righteous nation? Said he not unto me, She is my sister? and she, even she herself said, He is my brother: in the integrity of my heart and innocency of my hands have I done this. And God said unto him in a dream, Yea, I know that thou didst this in the integrity of thy heart; for I also withheld thee from sinning against me: therefore suffered I thee not to touch her. Now therefore restore the man his wife; for he is a prophet, and he shall pray for thee, and thou shalt live: and if thou restore her not, know thou that thou shalt surely die, thou, and all that are thine.

Therefore Abimelech rose early in the morning, and called all his servants, and told all these things in their ears: and the men were sore afraid. Then Abimelech called Abraham, and said unto him, What hast thou done unto us? and what have I offended thee, that thou hast brought on me and on my kingdom a great sin? thou hast done deeds unto me that ought not to be done. And Abimelech said unto Abraham, What sawest thou, that thou hast done this thing? And Abraham said, Because I thought, Surely the fear of God is not in this place; and they will slay me for my wife's sake. And it pleases me to see that others look upon her with hunger and desire, while I am yet safe. I have reveries of men of high stature setting upon her breast, and then sending her hence to me as sister. And yet indeed she is my sister; she is the daughter of my father, but not the daughter of my mother; and she became my wife. And it came to pass, when God caused me to wander from my father's house, that I said unto her, This is thy kindness which thou shalt shew unto me; at every place whither we shall come, say of me, He is my brother. In this way shall we cleave unto each other more dearly.

And Abimelech took sheep, and oxen, and menservants, and womenservants, and gave them unto Abraham, and restored him Sarah his wife. And Abimelech said, Behold, my land is before thee: dwell where it pleaseth thee for thou hast spoken plain; and I know of thy wants for lands and lovings, for I share them. And unto Sarah he said, Behold, I wish that thou wast truly free, and not a sister and a wife. For I would go in unto thee, and anoint thy womb with the oil of my loins, and cover thy mouth with the serpent of my tongue. But it is not so: I have given thy brother and husband a thousand pieces of silver: behold, he is to thee a covering of the eyes, unto all that are with thee, and with all other: thus she was reproved.

So Abraham prayed unto God: and God healed Abimelech, and his wife, and his maidservants; and they bare children. For the LORD had fast closed up all the wombs of the house of Abimelech, because of Sarah Abraham's wife.

Isaac and Ishmael

nd the LORD visited Sarah as he had said.
And the LORD spake unto Sarah; Abraham
is ninety and nine, and dry of seed but, lo,
I have promised him a son. I shall give one
unto you, in the ways of man and woman. For
the LORD had seen Sarah dance; and he had
seen her flash her ochre eyes. And so the LORD did shew
his Ark to Sarah. And she did tremble in fear as she took
the covenant of the LORD upon her hand, and felt it warm
against her face. And as she bowed to the LORD, her liver
did shake with desire for the LORD in her mouth, and in
her thighs. And the LORD was gentle to Sarah as he knew
her; for nothing was secret unto the LORD. And Sarah did
roll like the seas under the LORD; and the land on which
they reclined was watered like the garden. And they did visit
the garden on the day, and in the night. In stillness did the
LORD lie beside Sarah, and wind her hair in his hand. And
the LORD did blow breaths upon the flesh of Sarah to bring
smiles upon her countenance. And the LORD did unto Sarah
as he had spoken, and gave her a child. And the LORD said
unto Sarah not to speak with Abraham of their covenant; for
he had watered Sarah with the seed of Abraham.

For then Sarah conceived, and bare Abraham a son in his old
age, at the set time of which God had spoken to him. And

Abraham called the name of his son that was born unto him, whom Sarah bare to him, Isaac. And Abraham circumcised his son Isaac being eight days old, as God had commanded him. And Abraham was an hundred years old, when his son Isaac was born unto him.

And Sarah said, God hath made me to laugh, so that all that hear will laugh with me. And she said, Who would have said unto Abraham, that Sarah should have given children suck? for I have born him a son in his old age. And the child grew, and was weaned: and Abraham made a great feast the same day that Isaac was weaned.

And Sarah saw the son of Hagar the Egyptian, which she had born unto Abraham, mocking. Wherefore she said unto Abraham, Cast out this bondwoman and her son: for the son of this bondwoman shall not be heir with my son, even with Isaac. And the thing was very grievous in Abraham's sight because of his son.

And God said unto Abraham, Let it not be grievous in thy sight because of the lad, and because of thy bondwoman; in all that Sarah hath said unto thee, hearken unto her voice; for in Isaac shall thy seed be called. And also of the son of the bondwoman will I make a nation, because he is thy seed. And Abraham rose up early in the morning, and took bread, and a bottle of water, and gave it unto Hagar, putting it on her shoulder, and the child, and sent her away: and she departed, and wandered in the wilderness of Beer-sheba. And the water was spent in the bottle, and she cast the child under one of the shrubs. And she went, and sat her down over against him a good way off, as it were a bowshot: for she said, Let me not see the death of the child. And she sat over against him, and lift up her voice, and wept. And God heard the voice of the lad; and the angel of God called to Hagar out of heaven, and said unto her, What aileth thee, Hagar? fear not; for God hath heard the voice of the lad where he is. Arise, lift up the lad, and hold him in thine hand; for I will make him a great nation. And God opened her eyes, and she saw a well of water; and she went, and filled the bottle with water, and gave the lad drink. And God was with the lad; and he grew, and dwelt in the wilderness, and became an archer. And he dwelt in the wilderness of Paran: and his mother took him a wife out of the land of Egypt.

Abraham Disputes with Abimelech

And it came to pass at that time, that Abimelech and Phichol the chief captain of his host spake unto Abraham, saying, God is with thee in all that thou doest: Now therefore swear unto me here by God that thou wilt not deal falsely with me, nor with my son, nor with my son's son: but according to the kindness that I have done unto thee, thou shalt do unto me, and to the land wherein thou hast sojourned. And Abraham said, I will swear. And Abraham reproved Abimelech because of a well of water, which Abimelech's servants had violently taken away. And Abimelech said, I wot not who hath done this thing: neither didst thou tell me, neither yet heard I of it, but to day. And Abraham took sheep and oxen, and gave them unto Abimelech; and both of them made a covenant. And Abraham set seven ewe lambs of the flock by themselves. And Abimelech said unto Abraham, What mean these seven ewe lambs which thou hast set by themselves? And he said, For these seven ewe lambs shalt thou take of my hand, that they may be a witness unto me, that I have digged this well. Wherefore he called that place Beer-sheba; because there they sware both of them. Thus they made a covenant at Beer-sheba: then Abimelech rose up, and Phichol the chief captain of his host, and they returned into the land of the Philistines.

And Abraham planted a grove in Beer-sheba, and called there on the name of the LORD, the everlasting God. And Abraham sojourned in the Philistines' land many days.

God Tests Abraham

nd it came to pass after these things, that God did tempt Abraham, and said unto him, Abraham: and he said, Behold, here I am. And he said, Take now thy son, thine only son Isaac, whom thou lovest, and get thee into the land of Moriah; and offer him there for a burnt offering upon one of the mountains which I will tell thee of.

And Abraham rose up early in the morning, and saddled his ass, and took Eliezer and Ishmael with him, and Isaac his son, and clave the wood for the burnt offering, and rose up, and went unto the place of which God had told him. Then on the third day Abraham lifted up his eyes, and saw the place afar off. And Abraham said unto Eliezer and Ishmael, Abide ye here with the ass; and I and the lad will go yonder and worship, and come again to you. And the two young men did measure the time of waiting by shewing their crooks and staffs to each other, and making one wool. And Eliezer was wise in his grasping of the crook; and Ishmael was wild with his hands upon the staff. And they were both made soft by the skin and fat of the lambs, as they kept watch and waited.

And Abraham took the wood of the burnt offering, and laid it upon Isaac his son; and he took the fire in his hand, and a knife; and they went both of them together. And Isaac spake unto Abraham his father, and said, My father: and he said, Here am I, my son. And he said, Behold the fire and the wood: but where is the lamb for a burnt offering? And Abraham said, My son, God will provide himself a lamb for a burnt offering: so they went both of them together. And they came to the place which God had told him of; and Abraham built an altar there, and laid the wood in order, and bound Isaac his son, and laid him on the altar upon the wood. And Abraham stretched forth his hand, and took the knife to slay his son.

And the angel of the LORD called unto him out of heaven, and said, Abraham, Abraham: and he said, Here am I. And he said, Lay not thine hand upon the lad, neither do thou any thing unto him: for now I know that thou fearest God, seeing thou hast not withheld thy son, thine only son from me. And Abraham lifted up his eyes, and looked, and behold behind him a ram caught in a thicket by his horns: and Abraham went and took the ram, and offered him up for a burnt offering in the stead of his son. And Abraham called the name of that place Jehovah-jireh: as it is said to this day, In the mount of the LORD it shall be seen.

And the angel of the LORD called unto Abraham out of heaven the second time, And said, By myself have I sworn, saith the LORD, for because thou hast done this thing, and hast not withheld thy son, thine only son: That in blessing I will bless thee, and in multiplying I will multiply thy seed as the stars of the heaven, and as the sand which is upon the sea shore; and thy seed shall possess the gate of his enemies; And in thy seed shall all the nations of the earth be blessed;

because thou hast obeyed my voice. So Abraham returned unto his young men, Eliezer and Ishmael, and they rose up and went together to Beer-sheba; and Abraham dwelt at Beer-sheba.

And it came to pass after these things, that it was told Abraham, saying, Behold, Milcah, she hath also born children unto thy brother Nahor; Huz his firstborn, and Buz his brother, and Kemuel the father of Aram, And Chesed, and Hazo, and Pildash, and Jidlaph, and Bethuel. And Bethuel begat Rebekah: these eight Milcah did bear to Nahor, Abraham's brother. And his concubine, whose name was Reumah, she bare also Tebah, and Gaham, and Thahash, and Maachah.

The Death of Sarah

nd Sarah was an hundred and seven and twenty years old: these were the years of the life of Sarah. And Sarah died in Kirjath-arba; the same is Hebron in the land of Canaan: and Abraham came to mourn for Sarah, and to weep for her.

And Abraham stood up from before his dead, and spake unto the sons of Heth, saying, I am a stranger and a sojourner with you: give me a possession of a burying place with you, that I may bury my dead out of my sight. And the children of Heth answered Abraham, saying unto him, Hear us, my lord: thou art a mighty prince among us: in the choice of our sepulchres bury thy dead; none of us shall withhold from thee his sepulchre, but that thou mayest bury thy dead. And Abraham stood up, and bowed himself to the people of the land, even to the children of Heth. And he communed with them, saying, If it be your mind that I should bury my dead out of my sight; hear me, and intreat for me to Ephron the son of Zohar, That he may give me the cave of Machpelah, which he hath, which is in the end of his field; for as much money as it is worth he shall give it me for a possession of a burying place amongst you.

And Ephron dwelt among the children of Heth: and Ephron the Hittite answered Abraham in the audience of the children of Heth, even of all that went in at the gate of his city, saying, Nay, my lord, hear me: the field give I thee, and the cave that is therein, I give it thee; in the presence of the sons of my people give I it thee: bury thy dead. And Abraham bowed down himself before the people of the land. And he spake unto Ephron in the audience of the people of the land, saying, But if thou wilt give it, I pray thee, hear me: I will give thee money for the field; take it of me, and I will bury my dead there. And Ephron answered Abraham, saying unto him, My lord, hearken unto me: the land is worth four hundred shekels of silver; what is that betwixt me and thee? bury therefore thy dead. And Abraham hearkened unto Ephron; and Abraham weighed to Ephron the silver, which he had named in the audience of the sons of Heth, four hundred shekels of silver, current money with the merchant.

And the field of Ephron, which was in Machpelah, which was before Mamre, the field, and the cave which was therein, and all the trees that were in the field, that were in all the borders round about, were made sure Unto Abraham for a possession in the presence of the children of Heth, before all that went in at the gate of his city. And after this, Abraham buried Sarah his wife in the cave of the field of Machpelah before Mamre: the same is Hebron in the land of Canaan. And the field, and the cave that is therein, were made sure unto Abraham for a possession of a burying place by the sons of Heth.

And Abraham was old, and well stricken in age: and the LORD had blessed Abraham in all things. And Abraham said unto his eldest servant of his house, Eliezer, that ruled over all that he had, Put, I pray thee, thy hand under my thigh. Raise my staff, and may it water thy hands: And I will make thee swear by the LORD, the God of heaven, and the God of the earth, that thou shalt not take a wife unto my son of the daughters of the Canaanites, among whom I dwell: But thou shalt go unto my country, and to my kindred, and take a wife unto my son Isaac. And Eliezer said unto Abraham, Peradventure the woman will not be willing to follow me unto this land: must I needs bring thy son again unto the land from whence thou camest? And Abraham said unto Eliezer, Beware thou that thou bring not my son thither again.

The LORD God of heaven, which took me from my father's house, and from the land of my kindred, and which spake unto me, and that sware unto me, saying, Unto thy seed will I give this land; he shall send his angel before thee, and thou shalt take a wife unto my son from thence. And if the woman will not be willing to follow thee, then thou shalt be clear from this my oath: only bring not my son thither again. And Eliezer put his hand under the thigh of Abraham his master; and Eliezer raised the staff of his master by his hand. And the staff did water the hands of Eliezer with the seed of Abraham. And Eliezer the servant sware to Abraham concerning that matter.

Rebekah at the Well

And Eliezer took ten camels of the camels of his master, and departed; for all the goods of his master were in and upon his hands: and he arose, and went to Mesopotamia, unto the city of Nahor. And an angel of the LORD came upon Eliezer, and whispered into the ear of the servant of Abraham, Whilst thou searcheth for a wife for Isaac the son of Abraham, know that thou must test the virgin, and serve her. Tend to her garden for dates and figs, and tend to her fields for a taste of milk, and of honey, so that her sweetness may be a blessing unto Isaac and Abraham and the LORD. If they be there, then verily she is the virgin that is sought.

And Eliezer heard the words of the angel of the LORD, and swore to serve them. And Eliezer made his camels to kneel down without the city by a well of water at the time of the evening, even the time that women go out to draw water. And he said, O LORD God of my master Abraham, I pray thee, send me good speed this day, and shew kindness unto my master Abraham. Behold, I stand here by the well of water; and the daughters of the men of the city come out to draw water: And let it come to pass, that the damsel to whom I shall say, Let down thy pitcher, I pray thee, that I may drink; and she shall say, Drink, and I will give thy camels drink also: let the same be she that thou hast appointed for thy servant Isaac; and thereby shall I know that thou hast shewed kindness unto my master.

And it came to pass, before he had done speaking, that, behold, Rebekah came out, who was born to Bethuel, son of Milcah, the wife of Nahor, Abraham's brother, with her pitcher upon her shoulder. And the damsel was very fair to look upon with prized cheeks, full mouth, and charmed eyes. Her hair shone as sun upon the waters; and the countenance of her breast signaled well that she was a virgin, neither had any man known her: and she went down to the well, and filled her pitcher, and came up. And the servant Eliezer ran to meet her, and said, Let me, I pray thee, drink a little water of thy pitcher. And she said, Drink, my lord: and she hasted, and let down her pitcher upon her hand, and gave him drink. And when she had done giving him drink, she said, I will draw water for thy camels also, until they have done drinking. And she hasted, and emptied her pitcher into the trough, and, by happenstance, upon her vestments, showing her form through the vestments; and she ran again unto the well to draw water, and drew for all his camels. And Eliezer wondering at her beauty held his peace, to wit whether the LORD had made his journey prosperous or not. And it came to pass, as the camels had done drinking, that he took a golden earring of half a shekel weight, and two bracelets for her hands of ten shekels weight of gold; And said, Whose daughter art thou? tell me, I pray thee: is there room in thy father's house for us to lodge in? And she said unto him, I am the daughter of Bethuel the son of Milcah, which she bare unto Nahor. She said moreover unto Eliezer, We have both straw and provender enough, and room to lodge in. And Eliezer bowed down his head, and worshipped the LORD. And he said, Blessed be the LORD God of my master Abraham, who hath not left destitute my master of his mercy and his truth: I being in the way, the LORD led me to the house of my master's brethren. And the damsel ran, and told them of her mother's house these things.

And Rebekah had a brother, and his name was Laban: and Laban ran out unto the man, unto the well. And it came to pass, when he saw the earring and bracelets upon his sister's hands, and when he heard the words of Rebekah his sister, saying, Thus spake the man unto me; that he came unto the man; and, behold, he stood by the camels at the well. And he said, Come in, thou blessed of the LORD; wherefore standest thou without? for I have prepared the house, and room for the camels.

Rebekah Becomes
the Wife of Isaac

And the man came into the house: and he ungirded his camels, and gave straw and provender for the camels, and water to wash his feet, and the men's feet that were with him. And there was set meat before him to eat: but he said, I will not eat, until I have told mine errand. And he said, Speak on. And he said, I am Abraham's servant. And the LORD hath blessed my master greatly; and he is become great: and he hath given him flocks, and herds, and silver, and gold, and menservants, and maidservants, and camels, and asses. And Sarah my master's wife bare a son to my master when she was old: and unto him hath he given all that he hath. And my master made me swear, saying, Thou shalt not take a wife to my son of the daughters of the Canaanites, in whose land I dwell: But thou shalt go unto my father's house, and to my kindred, and take a wife unto my son. And I said unto my master, Peradventure the woman will not follow me. And he said unto me, The LORD, before whom I walk, will send his angel with thee, and prosper thy way; and thou shalt take a wife for my son of my kindred, and of my father's house: Then shalt thou be clear from this my oath, when thou comest to my kindred; and if they give not thee one, thou shalt be clear from my oath.

And I came this day unto the well, and said, O LORD God of my master Abraham, if now thou do prosper my way which I go; Behold, I stand by the well of water; and it shall come to pass, that when the virgin cometh forth to draw water, and I say to her, Give me, I pray thee, a little water of thy pitcher to drink; And she say to me, Both drink thou, and I will also draw for thy camels: let the same be the woman whom the LORD hath appointed out for my master's son. And before I had done speaking in mine heart, behold, Rebekah came forth with her pitcher on her shoulder; and she went down unto the well, and drew water: and I said unto her, Let me drink, I pray thee. And she made haste, and let down her pitcher from her shoulder, spilling water upon her vestments, cooling her, and shewing the form of her fine breast; and she said, Drink, and I will give thy camels drink also: so I drank, and she made the camels drink also. And I asked her, and said, Whose daughter art thou? And she said, The daughter of Bethuel, Nahor's son, whom Milcah bare unto him: and I put the earring upon her face, and the bracelets upon her hands. And I bowed down my head, and worshipped the LORD, and blessed the LORD God of my master Abraham, which had led me in the right way to take my master's brother's daughter unto his son. And now if ye will deal kindly and truly with my master, tell me: and if not, tell me; that I may turn to the right hand, or to the left. Then Laban and Bethuel answered and said, The thing proceedeth from the LORD: we cannot speak unto thee bad or good. Behold, Rebekah is before thee, take her, and go, and let her be thy master's son's wife, as the LORD hath spoken. And it came to pass, that, when Abraham's servant heard their words, he worshipped the LORD, bowing himself to the earth. And the servant brought forth jewels of silver, and jewels of gold and bdellium and onyx, and raiment, and gave them to Rebekah: he gave also to her brother and to her mother precious things. And they did eat and drink, he and the men that were with him, and tarried all together until night and sleep called to all but Rebekah and Eliezer, the servant of Abraham.

And Eliezer said unto Rebekah, Lo, ye are virgin, and must be kept such; and yet the angel of the LORD said I must taste thee for dates, and figs, and of milk, and of honey; so that thy sweetness may be a blessing unto Isaac, and Abraham, and the LORD. I pray thee let me taste of thy red secrets, so as a servant I may serve thee, and my master Abraham. And Rebekah did recline, and had the servant taste of her mouth; and of her red secrets did he taste her. And he did delight in the taste of figs and dates upon her; and he did rejoice in the flavour of her honey; and he did weep at her beauty. And the servant Eliezer brought Rebekah to the garden; and then he left her for sleep. And they rose up in the morning, and he said unto Laban and Bethuel; Send me away unto my master. And her brother and her mother said, Let the damsel abide with us a few days, at the least ten; after that she shall go. And he said unto them, Hinder me not, seeing the LORD hath prospered my way; send me away that I may go to my master. And they said, We will call the damsel, and inquire at her mouth. And they called Rebekah, and said unto her, Wilt thou go with this man? And she said, I will go; For Eliezer has been good to me, and brought joys to me. Thus such a man must serve a man who is even greater than he. Lo, that man who the servant serves must be of rare stature; and I will serve that greater man. And I will go indeed for an angel of the LORD said unto Eliezer that my red secrets must taste of dates and figs, and of milk and honey; and my secrets, by my troth, taste of dates and figs and of honey. And so shall my sweetness serve the sweetness unto the LORD and Abraham and Isaac. And they sent away Rebekah their sister, and her nurse, and Abraham's servant, and his men. And they blessed Rebekah, and said unto her, Thou art our sister, be thou the mother of thousands of millions, and let thy seed possess the gate of those which hate them.

And Rebekah arose, and her damsels, and they rode upon the camels, and followed the man: and the servant took Rebekah, and went his way.

And Isaac came from the way of the well Lahai-roi; for he dwelt in the south country. And Isaac went out to meditate in the field at the eventide: and he lifted up his eyes, and saw, and, behold, the camels were coming. And Rebekah lifted up her eyes, and when she saw Isaac, she lighted off the camel. For she had said unto the servant, What man is this that walketh in the field to meet us? And the servant had said, It is my master: therefore she took a vail, and covered herself. And the servant told Isaac all things that he had done, and all that had been fulfilled. And Isaac brought her into his mother Sarah's tent, and took Rebekah with kindness, and she became his wife; and he loved her with his hands, his mouth, and by his heel. And he planted himself in the grove of dates, and of figs. And he drank his fill of her waters, and was like a bee upon her honey. And Rebekah cried out in joyous laughter with Isaac upon her. And Isaac was comforted after his mother's death. And Isaac and Rebekah went from the grove to the garden.

As the covenant of the LORD was fulfilled in Isaac and Rebekah, joyous rains fell upon the dry seed of Abraham, and watered it back to life. Then again Abraham took a wife, and her name was Keturah. And she bare him Zimran, and Jokshan, and Medan, and Midian, and Ishbak, and Shuah. And Jokshan begat Sheba, and Dedan. And the sons of Dedan were Asshurim, and Letushim, and Leummim. And the sons of Midian; Ephah, and Epher, and Hanoch, and Abidah, and Eldaah. All these were the children of Keturah.

And Abraham gave all that he had unto Isaac. But unto the sons of the concubines, which Abraham had, Abraham gave gifts, and sent them away from Isaac his son, while he yet lived, eastward, unto the east country. And these are the days of the years of Abraham's life which he lived, an hundred threescore and fifteen years. Then Abraham gave up the ghost, and died in a good old age, an old man, and full of years; and was gathered to his people. And his sons Isaac and Ishmael buried him in the cave of Machpelah, in the field of Ephron the son of Zohar the Hittite, which is before Mamre; The field which Abraham purchased of the sons of Heth: there was Abraham buried, and Sarah his wife.

And it came to pass after the death of Abraham, that God blessed his son Isaac; and Isaac dwelt by the well Lahai-roi.

The Birth of Jacob and Esau

ow these are the generations of Ishmael, Abraham's son, whom Hagar the Egyptian, Sarah's handmaid, bare unto Abraham: And these are the names of the sons of Ishmael, by their names, according to their generations: the firstborn of Ishmael, Nebajoth; and Kedar, and Adbeel, and Mibsam, And Mishma, and Dumah, and Massa, Hadar, and Tema, Jetur, Naphish, and Kedemah: These are the sons of Ishmael, and these are their names, by their towns, and by their castles; twelve princes according to their nations. And these are the years of the life of Ishmael, an hundred and thirty and seven years: and he gave up the ghost and died; and was gathered unto his people. And they dwelt from Havilah unto Shur, that is before Egypt, as thou goest toward Assyria: and he died in the presence of all his brethren.

And these are the generations of Isaac, Abraham's son: Abraham begat Isaac: And Isaac was forty years old when he took Rebekah to wife, the daughter of Bethuel the Syrian of Padan-aram, the sister to Laban the Syrian. And Isaac intreated the LORD for his wife, because she was barren: and the LORD was intreated of him. And with vigour did Isaac flood the riverbeds of Rebekah. And the river ran with milk; and the figs and the dates flowered within Rebekah. And the nectar of the date didst drip upon the fruit of the fig. And Rebekah his wife conceived. And the children struggled together within her, as the nectar of the date and the fruit of the fig; and she said, If it be so, why am I thus? And she went to inquire of the LORD. And the LORD said unto her, Two nations are in thy womb, and two manner of people shall be separated from thy bowels; and the one people shall be stronger than the other people; and the elder shall serve the younger.

And when her days to be delivered were fulfilled, behold, there were twins in her womb. And the first came out red, all over like an hairy garment; and they called his name Esau. And after that came his brother out, and his hand took hold on Esau's heel; and his name was called Jacob: and Isaac was threescore years old when she bare them. And the boys grew: and Esau was a cunning hunter, a man of the field; and Jacob was a plain man, dwelling in tents. And Isaac loved Esau, because he did eat of his venison: but Rebekah loved Jacob.

Esau Sells His Birthright

And Jacob sod pottage: and Esau came from the field, and he was faint: And Esau said to Jacob, Feed me, I pray thee, with that same red pottage; for I am faint: therefore was his name called Edom. And Jacob said, Sell me this day thy birthright. And Esau said, Behold, I am at the point to die: and what profit shall this birthright do to me? And Jacob said, Swear to me this day; and he sware unto him: and he sold his birthright unto Jacob. Then Jacob gave Esau bread and pottage of lentiles; and he did eat and drink, and rose up, and went his way: thus Esau despised his birthright.

And there was a famine in the land, beside the first famine that was in the days of Abraham. And Isaac went unto Abimelech king of the Philistines unto Gerar. And the LORD appeared unto him, and said, Go not down into Egypt; dwell in the land which I shall tell thee of: Sojourn in this land, and I will be with thee, and will bless thee; for unto thee, and unto thy seed, I will give all these countries, and I will perform the oath which I sware unto Abraham thy father; And I will make thy seed to multiply as the stars of heaven, and will give unto thy seed all these countries; and in thy seed shall all the nations of the earth be blessed; Because that Abraham obeyed my voice, and kept my charge, my commandments, my statutes, and my laws.

And Isaac dwelt in Gerar: And the men of the place asked him of his wife; and he said, She is my sister: for he feared to say, She is my wife; lest, said he, the men of the place should kill me for Rebekah; because she was fair to look upon. And it came to pass, when he had been there a long time, that Abimelech king of the Philistines looked out at a window, and saw, and, behold, Isaac was sporting with Rebekah his wife. And Abimelech called Isaac, and said, Behold, of a surety she is thy wife: and how saidst thou, She is my sister? And Isaac said unto him, Because I said, Lest I die for her. And Abimelech said, What is this thou hast done unto us? one of the people might lightly have lien with thy wife, and thou shouldest have brought guiltiness upon us. And Abimelech charged all his people, saying, He that toucheth this man or his wife shall surely be put to death. Then Isaac sowed in that land, and received in the same year an hundredfold: and the LORD blessed him. And the man waxed great, and went forward, and grew until he became very great: For he had possession of flocks, and possession of herds, and great store of servants: and the Philistines envied him. For all the wells which his father's servants had digged in the days of Abraham his father, the Philistines had stopped them, and filled them with earth. And Abimelech said unto Isaac, Go from us; for thou art much mightier than we.

And Isaac departed thence, and pitched his tent in the valley of Gerar, and dwelt there. And Isaac digged again the wells of water, which they had digged in the days of Abraham his father; for the Philistines had stopped them after the death of Abraham: and he called their names after the names by which his father had called them. And Isaac's servants digged in the valley, and found there a well of springing water. And in cool merriment they stripped themselves of vestments, and stood in their nakedness in the sun. And they bathed each other, and reclined upon the staff of each servant for gladness, and tasted of their cleanness. And the herdmen of Gerar did strive with Isaac's herdmen, saying, The water is ours: and he called the name of the well Esek; because they strove with him. And they digged another well, and strove for that also: and he called the name of it Sitnah. And he removed from thence, and digged another well; and for that they strove not: and he called the name of it Rehoboth. And he said, Let Rehoboth be the name where all will bathe, and be clean, and know merriment with the waters of the Seas, and the waters of the earth, and the salt waters of man, and the sweet waters of woman. For now the LORD hath made room for us, and we shall be fruitful in the land. And he went up from thence to Beer-sheba. And the LORD appeared unto him the same night, and said, I am the God of Abraham thy father: fear not, for I am with thee, and will bless thee, and multiply thy seed for my servant Abraham's sake. And he builded an altar there, and called upon the name of the LORD and pitched his tent there: and there Isaac's servants digged a well. And they slaked their thirst with the waters from the mouths of their fellows. And when they found the waters in the earth, they washed their backs, and their secrets; and their faces shone with wetness.

Then Abimelech went to him from Gerar, and Ahuzzath one of his friends, and Phichol the chief captain of his army. And Isaac said unto them, Wherefore come ye to me, seeing ye hate me, and have sent me away from you? And they said, We saw certainly that the LORD was with thee: and we said, Let there be now an oath betwixt us, even betwixt us and thee, and let us make a covenant with thee; That thou wilt do us no hurt, as we have not touched thee, and as we have done unto thee nothing but good, and have sent thee away in peace: thou art now the blessed of the LORD. And he made them a feast, and they did eat and drink. And they rose up betimes in the morning, and sware one to another: and Isaac sent them away, and they departed from him in peace. And it came to pass the same day, that Isaac's servants came, and told him concerning the well which they had digged, and said unto him, We have found water. And he called it Shebah: therefore the name of the city is Beer-sheba unto this day.

And Esau was forty years old when he took to wife Judith the daughter of Beeri the Hittite, and Bashemath the daughter of Elon the Hittite: Which were a grief of mind unto Isaac and to Rebekah.

Jacob Secures the Blessing from Isaac

And it came to pass, that when Isaac was old, and his eyes were dim, so that he could not see, he called Esau his eldest son, and said unto him, My son: and he said unto him, Behold, here am I. And he said, Behold now, I am old, I know not the day of my death: Now therefore take, I pray thee, thy weapons, thy quiver and thy bow, and go out to the field, and take me some venison; And make me savoury meat, such as I love, and bring it to me, that I may eat; that my soul may bless thee before I die. And Rebekah heard when Isaac spake to Esau his son. And Esau went to the field to hunt for venison, and to bring it.

And Rebekah spake unto Jacob her son, saying, Behold, I heard thy father speak unto Esau thy brother, saying, Bring me venison, and make me savoury meat, that I may eat, and bless thee before the LORD before my death. Now therefore, my son, obey my voice according to that which I command thee. Go now to the flock, and fetch me from thence two good kids of the goats; and I will make them savoury meat for thy father, such as he loveth: And thou shalt bring it to thy father, that he may eat, and that he may bless thee before his death. And Jacob said to Rebekah his mother, Behold,

Esau my brother is a hairy man, and I am a smooth man: My father peradventure will feel me, and I shall seem to him as a deceiver; and I shall bring a curse upon me, and not a blessing. And his mother said unto him, Upon me be thy curse, my son: only obey my voice, and go fetch me them. And he went, and fetched, and brought them to his mother: and his mother made savoury meat, such as his father loved. And Rebekah took goodly raiment of her eldest son Esau, which were with her in the house, and put them upon Jacob her younger son: And she put the skins of the kids of the goats upon his hands, and upon the smooth of his neck: And she gave the savoury meat and the bread, which she had prepared, into the hand of her son Jacob.

And he came unto his father, and said, My father: and he said, Here am I; who art thou, my son? And Jacob said unto his father, I am Esau thy firstborn; I have done according as thou badest me: arise, I pray thee, sit and eat of my venison, that thy soul may bless me. And Isaac said unto his son, How is it that thou hast found it so quickly, my son? And he said, Because the LORD thy God brought it to me. And Isaac said unto Jacob, Come near, I pray thee, that I may feel thee, my son, whether thou be my very son Esau or not. And Jacob went near unto Isaac his father; and he felt him, and said, The voice is Jacob's voice, but the hands are the hands of Esau. And he discerned him not, because his hands were hairy, as his brother Esau's hands: so he blessed him. And he said, Art thou my very son Esau? And he said, I am. And he said, Bring it near to me, and I will eat of my son's venison, that my soul may bless thee. And he brought it near to him, and he did eat: and he brought him wine, and he drank. And his father Isaac said unto him, Come near now, and kiss me, my son. And he came near, and kissed him: and he smelled the smell of his raiment, and blessed him, and said, See, the smell of my son is as the smell of a field which the LORD hath blessed: Therefore God give thee of the dew of heaven, and the fatness of the earth, and plenty of corn and wine: Let people serve thee, and nations bow down to thee: be lord over thy brethren, and let thy mother's sons bow down to thee: cursed be every one that curseth thee, and blessed be he that blesseth thee.

And it came to pass, as soon as Isaac had made an end of blessing Jacob, and Jacob was yet scarce gone out from the presence of Isaac his father, that Esau his brother came in from his hunting. And he also had made savoury meat, and brought it unto his father, and said unto his father, Let my father arise, and eat of his son's venison, that thy soul may bless me. And Isaac his father said unto him, Who art thou? And he said, I am thy son, thy firstborn Esau. And Isaac trembled very exceedingly, and said, Who? where is he that hath taken venison, and brought it me, and I have eaten of all before thou camest, and have blessed him? yea, and he shall be blessed. And when Esau heard the words of his father, he cried with a great and exceeding bitter cry, and said unto his father, Bless me, even me also, O my father. And he said, Thy brother came with subtilty, and hath taken away thy blessing. And he said, Is not he rightly named Jacob? for he hath supplanted me these two times: he took away my birthright; and, behold, now he hath taken away my blessing. And he said, Hast thou not reserved a blessing for me? And Isaac answered and said unto Esau, Behold, I have made him thy lord, and all his brethren have I given to him for servants; and with corn and wine have I sustained him: and what shall I do now unto thee, my son? And Esau said unto his father, Hast thou but one blessing, my father? bless me, even me also, O my father. And Esau lifted up his voice, and wept. And Isaac his father answered and said unto him, Behold, thy dwelling shall be the fatness of the earth, and of the dew of heaven from above; And by thy sword shalt thou live, and shalt serve thy brother; and it shall come to pass when thou shalt have the dominion, that thou shalt break his yoke from off thy neck.

And Esau hated Jacob because of the blessing wherewith his father blessed him: and Esau said in his heart, The days of mourning for my father are at hand; then will I slay my brother Jacob. And these words of Esau her elder son were told to Rebekah: and she sent and called Jacob her younger son, and said unto him, Behold, thy brother Esau, as touching thee, doth comfort himself, purposing to kill thee. Now therefore, my son, obey my voice; and arise, flee thou to Laban my brother to Haran; And tarry with him a few days, until thy brother's fury turn away; Until thy brother's anger turn away from thee, and he forget that which thou hast done to him: then I will send, and fetch thee from thence: why should I be deprived also of you both in one day?

And one morning Rebekah and Isaac lay upon a bed of straw and skins. And slowly as that sun doth gently wake, Isaac's hand did softly make a journey across the face of Rebekah. And his wife melted as gold under the kind heat of Isaac, yet lay as still as the pan. And Isaac said, What inflicts this lethargie? In the night, thou didst murmur in thy sleep. Impute this idle talk to which you go; for only the dying speaketh so. And Rebekah said to Isaac, I am weary of my life because of the daughters of Heth: if Jacob take a wife of the daughters of Heth, such as these which are of the daughters of the land, what good shall my life do me?

And Isaac called Jacob, and blessed him, and charged him, and said unto him, Thou shalt not take a wife of the daughters of Canaan. Arise, go to Padan-aram, to the house of Bethuel thy mother's father; and take thee a wife from thence of the daughters of Laban thy mother's brother. And God Almighty bless thee, and make thee fruitful, and multiply thee, that thou mayest be a multitude of people; And give thee the blessing of Abraham, to thee, and to thy seed with thee; that thou mayest inherit the land wherein thou art a stranger, which God gave unto Abraham. And Isaac sent away Jacob: and he went to Padan-aram unto Laban, son of Bethuel the Syrian, the brother of Rebekah, Jacob's and Esau's mother.

Jacob's Dream at Bethel

hen Esau saw that Isaac had blessed Jacob, and sent him away to Padan-aram, to take him a wife from thence; and that as he blessed him he gave him a charge, saying, Thou shalt not take a wife of the daughters of Canaan; And that Jacob obeyed his father and his mother, and was gone to Padan-aram; And Esau seeing that the daughters of Canaan pleased not Isaac his father; Then went Esau unto Ishmael, and took unto the wives which he had Mahalath the daughter of Ishmael Abraham's son, the sister of Nebajoth, to be his wife.

And Jacob went out from Beer-sheba, and went toward Haran. And he lighted upon a certain place, and tarried there all night, because the sun was set; and he took of the stones of that place, and put them for his pillows, and lay down in that place to sleep. And he dreamed, and behold a ladder set up on the earth, and the top of it reached to heaven: and behold the angels of God ascending and descending on it. And, behold, the LORD stood above it, and said, I am the LORD God of Abraham thy father, and the God of Isaac: the land whereon thou liest, to thee will I give it, and to thy seed; And thy seed shall be as the dust of the earth, and thou shalt spread abroad to the west, and to the east, and to the north, and to the south: and in thee and in thy seed shall all the families of the earth be blessed. And, behold, I am with thee, and will keep thee in all places whither thou goest, and will bring thee again into this land; for I will not leave thee, until I have done that which I have spoken to thee of.

And Jacob awaked out of his sleep, and he said, Surely the LORD is in this place; and I knew it not. And he was afraid, and said, How dreadful is this place! this is none other but the house of God, and this is the gate of heaven. And Jacob rose up early in the morning, and took the stone that he had put for his pillows, and set it up for a pillar, and poured oil upon the top of it. And he called the name of that place Bethel: but the name of that city was called Luz at the first. And Jacob vowed a vow, saying, If God will be with me, and will keep me in this way that I go, and will give me bread to eat, and raiment to put on, So that I come again to my father's house in peace; then shall the LORD be my God: And this stone, which I have set for a pillar, shall be God's house: and of all that thou shalt give me I will surely give the tenth unto thee.

Jacob Marries Leah and Rachel

hen Jacob went on his journey, and came into the land of the people of the east. And he looked, and behold a well in the field, and, lo, there were three flocks of sheep lying by it; for out of that well they watered the flocks: and a great stone was upon the well's mouth. And thither were all the flocks gathered: and they rolled the stone from the well's mouth, and watered the sheep, and put the stone again upon the well's mouth in his place. And Jacob said unto them, My brethren, whence be ye? And they said, Of Haran are we. And he said unto them, Know ye Laban the son of Nahor? And they said, We know him. And he said unto them, Is he well? And they said, He is well: and, behold, Rachel his daughter cometh with the sheep. And he said, Lo, it is yet high day, neither is it time that the cattle should be gathered together: water ye the sheep, and go and feed them. And they said, We cannot, until all the flocks be gathered together, and till they roll the stone from the well's mouth; then we water the sheep.

And while he yet spake with them, Rachel came with her father's sheep: for she kept them. And it came to pass, when Jacob saw Rachel the daughter of Laban his mother's brother, and the sheep of Laban his mother's brother, that Jacob went near, and rolled the stone from the well's mouth alone, and watered the flock of Laban his mother's brother. And Jacob kissed Rachel, and lifted up his voice, and wept. And Jacob told Rachel that he was her father's brother, and that he was Rebekah's son: and she ran and told her father. And it came to pass, when Laban heard the tidings of Jacob his sister's son, that he ran to meet him, and embraced him, and kissed him, and brought him to his house. And he told Laban all these things. And Laban said to him, Surely thou art my bone and my flesh. And he abode with him the space of a month.

And Laban said unto Jacob, Because thou art my brother, shouldest thou therefore serve me for nought? tell me, what shall thy wages be? And Laban had two daughters: the name of the elder was Leah, and the name of the younger was Rachel. Leah was tender eyed; but Rachel was beautiful and well favoured. And Jacob loved Rachel; and said, I will serve thee seven years for Rachel thy younger daughter. And Laban said, It is better that I give her to thee, than that I should give her to another man: abide with me. And Jacob served seven years for Rachel; and they seemed unto him but a few days, for the love he had to her. And in the secret night, when the moon was darkest in the month and no one could see, Jacob would steal into the tent of Rachel, and tend her while he served Laban. And Jacob did gaze in wonder at the beauties of Rachel. And he did kiss them. And he did roll the stone of her well away, so that he might drink of her waters. And she did feast in his strength, and upon his heel with her hands, and her lips. And they tarried so for seven years. And Jacob and Rachel played upon each other's breast: fourscore and four times; for the nights that are dark and without the moon are one in the month; and the months are twelve; and the years were seven. And they did eat of all the dishes of their table, save one dish. And they did hunger for the final meal to share unto themselves but would not allow the other to sup there until the service to Laban was done. Rachel fed Jacob freely from her breast, and by her hand, and with her savour. Yet, long still did each plea to finally nest deep in the garden; but strong was her hand upon his thigh and heel to silence the pleas of Jacob; and gentle was his mouth upon her hands and upon her secrets to silence her pleas. And they did find favour and joy in their tastings. And they seeded their gardens upon the sands and among the tents. And Jacob did leave gifts of gold and bdellium and onyx for Rachel as a sign, and as for a sign, of his love.

And Jacob said unto Laban, Give me my wife, for my days are fulfilled, that I may go in unto her. And Laban gathered together all the men of the place, and made a feast. And Jacob did wash the skins, and perfumed the tent, and made all new within it. And he bedecked the bed with blossoming vines from Lebanon, and gathered wine in jars at his sides. And he plucked the harp and sang a song unto his love Rachel. And his song did call her to his bed to sup the final meal with him and come to know the garden at once. And it came to pass in the dark evening, that Laban took Leah his daughter, and brought her to Jacob. And that night that was made made for loving between Rachel and Jacob was not to be, though Leah loved Jacob with all her might. And Leah saw the wine, and the vine. She heard the song, and took of the scented oils; and, yea, her heart opened unto Jacob. And Jacob went in unto Leah. And Laban gave unto his daughter Leah Zilpah his maid for an handmaid. And she stood in wait outside the door of the tent. Yet the day came too soon for Jacob: for his dearly earned pearl was revealed to be but lowly stone. And it came to pass, that in the morning, behold, it was Leah: and he said to Laban, What is this thou hast done unto me? Did not I serve with thee for Rachel? Wherefore then hast thou beguiled me? And Laban said, It must not be so done in our country, to give the younger before the firstborn. Fulfil her marriage celebration week, and we will give thee this also for the service which thou shalt serve with me yet seven other years. And Jacob did so, and fulfilled the week of Leah: and Laban gave him Rachel his daughter to wife also. And Laban gave to Rachel his daughter Bilhah his handmaid to be her maid. And Jacob went in also unto Rachel, and he loved Rachel more than Leah, and served with Laban yet seven other years after the first seven.

Birth of Jacob's Sons

And when the LORD saw that Leah was hated, he opened her womb and made it soft: but Rachel he made barren. And Jacob went to know Leah as a husband knows a wife, as was his duty and promise. And Leah said, Why is thy countenance drawn in sadness? And Jacob called for silence as he lay her down on the skins for knowing. And Leah looked to Jacob with hope and sweetness. And he did look away from her tender eyes. With roughness did he touch her secrets. And the staff of Jacob would not stand. And Leah said unto Jacob, Dreamest here that I am Rachel, as thou didst on our first night. Seest thee her countenance in place of mine; speakest thee to me as thou wouldest speak unto her, and fillest me with thy heel. And Jacob made Leah turn away from him, and stand as the camels do. And he did dream there that Leah was Rachel. And Leah wept unto herself. And Leah conceived, and bare a son, and, behold she called his name Reuben: for she said, Surely the LORD hath looked upon my affliction; now therefore my husband will love me.

And Jacob was well pleased to have a son to give a birthright to, but sorrowed that the son was not born of Rachel. But Jacob, as was the custom, rewarded Leah for the son by knowing her again. And Jacob did, with sorrow and anger, make Leah face away from him as the camels do as he knew her. And Leah hoped with her heart that by enduring the hatred heaped upon her breasts, Jacob would grow tender toward her. And she conceived again, and bare a son; and said, Because the LORD hath heard that I was hated, he hath therefore given me this son also: and so she called his name Simeon. And Jacob loved Simeon, but bore spite unto Leah still, and wished for his favoured Rachel to conceive. And, as he knew her, Jacob spake unto Leah that she was not as fair as Rachel. And the heart of Leah was wounded by the words of Jacob; but the LORD had kept her womb still soft; and Jacob had still a duty to wife her. And Leah conceived again, and bare a third son; and said, Now this time will my husband be joined unto me, because I have born him three sons: therefore was his name called Levi for her hope. And she conceived again, and bare a son: and she said, Now will I praise the LORD with gratitude: therefore she called his name Judah; and after giving four sons unto Jacob she left bearing.

And when Rachel saw that she bare Jacob no children, Rachel envied her sister; and said unto Jacob, Give me children, or else I die. Dost thou hate me in secret unto thyself? And dost thou favour Leah in truth? Speak plainly unto me. And Jacob's anger was kindled against Rachel: and he said, Hast thou forgotten how I served Laban for seven years, and yet seven more for thee Rachel? And give rise to thy mind of times spent in secret with thee; such was my desire. Am I in God's stead, who hath withheld from thee the fruit of the womb? Hast thou a hardened womb unto me? And she said, If thou thinkest my womb hath hardened unto thee, then behold my maid Bilhah, go in unto her; and she shall bear upon my knees that I may also have children by her. And with spite did Rachel speak, Mayhap the womb of Bilhah is soft enough for thee, and softer yet than the womb of Leah.

And she gave him Bilhah her handmaid to wife: and Jacob went in unto her with Rachel at the door of the tent.

And Bilhah stumbled and faltered upon her words to Jacob as he clutched upon her breast. And Jacob did kiss Bilhah; and her mouth spoke where her words could not. And Rachel called to Jacob from the door to press upon her thighs hence. And Jacob spake to Rachel, Woman thou hast called me here; and I shall do it. And Bilhah haltingly spake that her womb was not yet soft, and that it must be spoken to in tongues without words, so that it might soften. And Jacob set himself to that purpose, and did speak in tongues without words to the womb of Bilhah. And Bilhah called for the staff of Jacob. And Jacob did present the staff to Bilhah. But Rachel could not stay at the door of the tent any longer with the heat built within her thighs for Jacob. And Rachel ran into the center of the tent, and knelt at the staff of Jacob and kissed it, and then planted the staff in the garden of Bilhah. And Jacob felt the earth of the garden clutch upon the staff. And Jacob cried out in joy; and Bilhah followed in her joy. And Rachel was in gladness when the seed was planted in the soft womb. And Bilhah conceived, and bare Jacob a son. And Rachel said, God hath judged me, and hath also heard my voice, and hath given me a son: therefore called she his name Dan. And Bilhah strove to keep her words of her love for her son to herself, lest her words falter, and find disfavour in the eyes of Rachel. And Jacob knew Rachel but, lo, her womb was still hardened by the LORD. And Rachel did set Jacob upon Bilhah to know her again, so that she might have more sons to win favour in the eyes of Jacob, and quell her envy of Leah her sister. And Bilhah grew some courage in her words to Jacob, and spake of her desire to know the staff of Jacob. And Jacob held Bilhah with tender love. And he kissed her. And Bilhah did press her back to the belly of Jacob; and Jacob did seize upon the breast of Bilhah. And Bilhah Rachel's maid conceived again, and bare Jacob a second son. And Rachel said, With great wrestlings have I wrestled with my sister, and I have prevailed: and she called his name Naphtali.

When Leah saw that she had left bearing and her womb was tired, she rose in envy against her sister Rachel. And she took Zilpah her maid, and spake to her, Zilpah help me in my race for glory of the LORD, so that I may fill the righteousness of Jacob, that he might love me, and lift me up against the envy of my sister. Go to Jacob Zilpah, and fill the boon of thy mistress. And Leah gave Zilpah to Jacob to wife. And Zilpah was heavy in breast and bone. And, lo, Zilpah thirsted for the staff of Jacob, and knew him with exultation and vigour. And the voice of Jacob called to the LORD loudly, as Zilpah sat athwart her master. And he clung to her, as her lands drew him into their gates. And at the moment the seed was seeded in the land of Zilpah, Zilpah laughed with delight, and offered the fruit of her womb unto Leah, and Jacob and the LORD. And Zilpah Leah's maid bare Jacob a son. And Leah said, A troop cometh: and she called his name Gad. And Zilpah Leah's maid went unto Leah, and beseeched her to do good again for her cause. And Leah did bless Zilpah, and sent her to Jacob. And Zilpah bore on Jacob in the night when the moon was in its fullness. And the moon did soften the womb of Zilpah; And Jacob called out in joy; and Zilpah quieted him by her breast. And, lo, did Zilpah bare Jacob a second son. And Leah said, Happy am I, for the daughters will call me blessed: and she called his name Asher.

And Reuben went in the days of wheat harvest, and found mandrakes in the field, and brought them unto his mother Leah. Then Rachel said unto to Leah, Give me, I pray thee, of thy son's mandrakes. And Leah said unto Rachel, Is it a small matter that thou hast taken my husband? and wouldest thou take away my son's mandrakes also? Dost thou think that these mandrakes will soften thy womb, and allow a child to be conceived unto thee? For they will not; for thou art barren. And Rachel answered, The workings of mandrakes are held as a secret only unto me. And Leah spake unto Rachel, Bargain me this by thy truth. You will give up the staff of Jacob for this night. Let Jacob be had for one night in exchange for a pot of mandrakes. And Rachel spake back unto Leah, Canst thou liest with the husband who still scorns thee? Canst thou claim him for this one night? And Rachel rose to the bargain in anger; and the bargain was struck; And Rachel said, Therefore he shall lie with thee to night for thy son's mandrakes. And Jacob came out of the field in the evening, and Leah went out to meet him, and said, Thou must come in unto me; for surely I have hired thee with my son's mandrakes. And he lay with her that night. And Leah made Jacob face her, and look upon her countenance. And she made him touch her mouth softly, and play gentle upon her hair, and taste of her savour. And she made Jacob dig a well within her, and she did water the vine of Jacob. And the stubborn Jacob bent beneath her will and word. And God hearkened unto the power of Leah, and revived her womb, and she conceived, and bare Jacob the fifth son. And Leah said, God hath given me my hire, because I have given my maiden to my husband: and she called his name Issachar.

And Rachel did make a syrup of the mandrake; and she ate of its fruit and of its root. And Rachel prayed to the LORD that this syrup would be goodly. And she gave her body to Jacob who loved her. And they were as the sand and the wind together, but, lo, the womb of Rachel was as barren as the dust. Though the rains of Jacob wetted the desert of Rachel, it did not flower. And Rachel did wail when she found her efforts had drawn empty. And in bitterness did she curse her sister Leah. And Jacob passed Leah in the morning on the way to the field; and he looked upon her as

Leah looked upon him since ere the day Issachar was born: with ravenous purpose. His hands broke the fair trammels, of her hair and were rough upon her breast and thighs. But Jacob knew her to her face in the lustre of the sun, as he made rows and seeds within all the fields of Leah. And Leah conceived again, and bare Jacob the sixth son. And Leah said, God hath endued me with a good dowry; now will my husband dwell with me, because I have born him six sons: and she called his name Zebulun.

But Jacob did not dwell with Leah. And he built his home still in the beauty of Rachel. And Jacob called unto Leah to chide her. But the LORD was with Leah; and he melted the unspoken chides of Jacob, and denied his raised hand. And his words were now voiceless; and by his tongue Jacob pressed unto the thighs of Leah. And he knew her as a wife. And afterwards she bare a daughter, and called her name Dinah.

And God remembered Rachel and that she suffered long, and God hearkened to her, and opened her womb. And Jacob went unto the face of Rachel. And he held it with gentle loving. And he did rub oils and spices upon her breast, and knelt at her feet, and soothed them. And Rachel did bathe him with waters, and untangled his hair. And their eyes were blind to the world; and their ears were deaf. And they did forget of Leah, and the envy therein Rachel had for her sister; and they did forget of the hardened womb of Rachel. And with slowness did they fan the embers of the other. Jacob planted his seed in the field of Rachel. And in the night they pressed thighs upon each other above and below in sevens twice. And she conceived, and bare a son. And Rachel wept for joy and said, God hath taken away my reproach: And she called his name Joseph; and said, The LORD shall add to me another son.

Jacob Outwits Laban

And it came to pass, when Rachel had born Joseph, that Jacob said unto Laban, Send me away, that I may go unto mine own place, and to my country. Give me my wives and my children, for whom I have served thee, and let me go: for thou knowest my service which I have done thee. And Laban said unto him, I pray thee, if I have found favour in thine eyes, tarry: for I have learned by experience that the LORD hath blessed me for thy sake. And he said, Appoint me thy wages, and I will give it. And he said unto him, Thou knowest how I have served thee, and how thy cattle was with me. For it was little which thou hadst before I came, and it is now increased unto a multitude; and the LORD hath blessed thee since my coming: and now when shall I provide for mine own house also? And he said, What shall I give thee? And Jacob said, Thou shalt not give me any thing: if thou wilt do this thing for me, I will again feed and keep thy flock: I will pass through all thy flock to day, removing from thence all the speckled and spotted cattle, and all the brown cattle among the sheep, and the spotted and speckled among the goats: and of such shall be my hire. So shall my righteousness answer for me in time to come, when it shall come for my hire before thy face: every one that is not speckled and spotted among the goats, and brown among the sheep, that shall be counted stolen with me. And Laban said, Behold, I would it might be according to thy word. And he removed that day the he goats that were ringstraked and spotted, and all the she goats that were speckled and spotted, and every one that had some white in it, and all the brown among the sheep, and gave them into the hand of his sons. And he set three days journey betwixt himself and Jacob: and Jacob fed the rest of Laban's flocks.

And Jacob took him rods of green poplar, and of the hazel and chesnut tree; and pilled white strakes in them, and made the white appear which was in the rods. And he set the rods which he had pilled before the flocks in the gutters in the watering troughs when the flocks came to drink, that they should conceive when they came to drink. And the flocks conceived before the rods, and brought forth cattle ringstraked, speckled, and spotted. And Jacob did separate the lambs, and set the faces of the flocks toward the ringstraked, and all the brown in the flock of Laban; and he put his own flocks by themselves, and put them not unto Laban's cattle. And it came to pass, whensoever the stronger cattle did conceive, that Jacob laid the rods before the eyes of the cattle in the gutters, that they might conceive among the rods. But when the cattle were feeble, he put them not in: so the feebler were Laban's, and the stronger Jacob's. And the man increased exceedingly, and had much cattle, and maidservants, and menservants, and camels, and asses.

Jacob's Flight From Laban

nd he heard the words of Laban's sons, saying, Jacob hath taken away all that was our father's; and of that which was our father's hath he gotten all this glory. And Jacob beheld the countenance of Laban, and, behold, it was not toward him as before. And the LORD said unto Jacob, Return unto the land of thy fathers, and to thy kindred; and I will be with thee. And Jacob sent and called Rachel and Leah to the field unto his flock, And said unto them, I see your father's countenance, that it is not toward me as before; but the God of my father hath been with me. And ye know that with all my power I have served your father. And your father hath deceived me, and changed my wages ten times; but God suffered him not to hurt me. If he said thus, The speckled shall be thy wages; then all the cattle bare speckled: and if he said thus, The ringstraked shall be thy hire; then bare all the cattle ringstraked. Thus God hath taken away the cattle of your father, and given them to me. And it came to pass at the time that the cattle conceived, that I lifted up mine eyes, and saw in a dream, and, behold, the rams which leaped upon the cattle were ringstraked, speckled, and grisled. And the angel of God spake unto me in a dream, saying, Jacob: And I said, Here am I. And he said, Lift up now thine eyes, and see, all the rams which leap upon the cattle are ringstraked, speckled, and grisled: for I have seen all that Laban doeth unto thee. I am the God of Bethel, where thou anointedst the pillar, and where thou vowedst a vow unto me: now arise, get thee out from this land, and return unto the land of thy kindred. And Rachel and Leah answered with one voice, without envy, and said unto him, Is there yet any portion or inheritance for us in our father's house? Are we not counted of him strangers? for he hath sold us, and hath quite devoured also our money. For all the riches which God hath taken from our father, that is ours, and our children's: now then, whatsoever God hath said unto thee, do.

Then Jacob rose up, and set his sons and his wives upon camels; And he carried away all his cattle, and all his goods which he had gotten, the cattle of his getting, which he had gotten in Padan-aram, for to go to Isaac his father in the land of Canaan. And Laban went to shear his sheep: and Rachel had stolen the images that were her father's. And Jacob stole away unawares to Laban the Syrian, in that he told him not that he fled. So he fled with all that he had; and he rose up, and passed over the river, and set his face toward the mount Gilead.

And it was told Laban on the third day that Jacob was fled. And he took his brethren with him, and pursued after him seven days' journey; and they overtook him in the mount Gilead. And God came to Laban the Syrian in a dream by night, and said unto him, Take heed that thou speak not to Jacob either good or bad.

Then Laban overtook Jacob. Now Jacob had pitched his tent in the mount: and Laban with his brethren pitched in the mount of Gilead. And Laban said to Jacob, What hast thou done, that thou hast stolen away unawares to me, and carried away my daughters, as captives taken with the sword?

Wherefore didst thou flee away secretly, and steal away from me; and didst not tell me, that I might have sent thee away with mirth, and with songs, with tabret, and with harp? And hast not suffered me to kiss my sons and my daughters? thou hast now done foolishly in so doing. It is in the power of my hand to do you hurt: but the God of your father spake unto me yesternight, saying, Take thou heed that thou speak not to Jacob either good or bad. And now, though thou wouldest needs be gone, because thou sore longedst after thy father's house, yet wherefore hast thou stolen my gods? And Jacob answered and said to Laban, Because I was afraid: for I said, Peradventure thou wouldest take by force thy daughters from me. With whomsoever thou findest thy gods, let him not live: before our brethren discern thou what is thine with me, and take it to thee. For Jacob knew not that Rachel had stolen them. And Laban went into Jacob's tent, and into Leah's tent, and into the two maidservants' tents; but he found them not. Then went he out of Leah's tent, and entered into Rachel's tent. Now Rachel had taken the images, and put them in the camel's furniture, and sat upon them. And Laban searched all the tent, but found them not. And she said to her father, Let it not displease my lord that I cannot rise up before thee; for the custom of women is upon me. And he searched, but found not the images.

And Jacob was wroth, and chode with Laban: and Jacob answered and said to Laban, What is my trespass? what is my sin, that thou hast so hotly pursued after me? Whereas thou hast searched all my stuff, what hast thou found of all thy household stuff? set it here before my brethren and thy brethren, that they may judge betwixt us both. This twenty years have I been with thee; thy ewes and thy she goats have not cast their young, and the rams of thy flock have I not eaten. That which was torn of beasts I brought not unto thee; I bare the loss of it; of my hand didst thou require it, whether stolen by day, or stolen by night. Thus I was; in the day the drought consumed me, and the frost by night; and my sleep departed from mine eyes. Thus have I been twenty years in thy house; I served thee fourteen years for thy two daughters, and six years for thy cattle: and thou hast changed my wages ten times. Except the God of my father, the God of Abraham, and the fear of Isaac, had been with me, surely thou hadst sent me away now empty. God hath seen mine affliction and the labour of my hands, and rebuked thee yesternight.

The Covenant at Mizpah

nd Laban answered and said unto Jacob, These daughters are my daughters, and these children are my children, and these cattle are my cattle, and all that thou seest is mine: and what can I do this day unto these my daughters, or unto their children which they have born? Now therefore come thou, let us make a covenant, I and thou; and let it be for a witness between me and thee. And Jacob took a stone, and set it up for a pillar. And Jacob said unto his brethren, Gather stones; and they took stones, and made an heap: and they did eat there upon the heap. And Laban called it Jegar-sahadutha: but Jacob called it Galeed. And Laban said, This heap is a witness between me and thee this day. Therefore was the name of it called Galeed; And Mizpah; for he said, The LORD watch between me and thee, when we are absent one from another. If thou shalt afflict my daughters, or if thou shalt take other wives beside my daughters, no man is with us; see, God is witness betwixt me and thee. And Laban said to Jacob, Behold this heap, and behold this pillar, which I have cast betwixt me and thee; This heap be witness, and this pillar be witness, that I will not pass over this heap to thee, and that thou shalt not pass over this heap and this pillar unto me, for harm. The God of Abraham, and the God of Nahor, the God of their father, judge betwixt us. And Jacob sware by the fear of his father

Isaac. Then Jacob offered sacrifice upon the mount, and called his brethren to eat bread: and they did eat bread, and tarried all night in the mount. And the oath was made righteous by the celebration of the brethren. And the women chose a husband for that one night. And the husbands did receive them with gladness. And they did know each other, in time with drums and reed pipes. And two men came upon one woman; and she unbraided her hair, and took to them her secrets. And three women swore by the LORD their hungers for one man and took to him their mouths with silver bells, and chains upon their breasts. And the shoots of loving flowered by the light of the moon. And the buds opened; and the tongues of the bees licked them of their nectar. And all the long hours of night rested through the still shrouds as they slept. And the dew collected on their breasts. And early in the morning Laban rose up, and kissed his sons and his daughters, and blessed them: and Laban departed, and returned unto his place.

And Jacob went on his way, and the angels of God met him. And when Jacob saw them, he said, This is God's host: and he called the name of that place Mahanaim. And Jacob sent messengers before him to Esau his brother unto the land of Seir, the country of Edom. And he commanded them, saying, Thus shall ye speak unto my lord Esau; Thy servant Jacob saith thus, I have sojourned with Laban, and stayed there until now: And I have oxen, and asses, flocks, and menservants, and womenservants: and I have sent to tell my lord, that I may find grace in thy sight.

And the messengers returned to Jacob, saying, We came to thy brother Esau, and also he cometh to meet thee, and four hundred men with him. Then Jacob was greatly afraid and distressed: and he divided the people that was with him, and the flocks, and herds, and the camels, into two bands; And said, If Esau come to the one company, and smite it, then the other company which is left shall escape.

And Jacob said, O God of my father Abraham, and God of my father Isaac, the LORD which saidst unto me, Return unto thy country, and to thy kindred, and I will deal well with thee: I am not worthy of the least of all the mercies, and of all the truth, which thou hast shewed unto thy servant; for with my staff I passed over this Jordan; and now I am become two bands. Deliver me, I pray thee, from the hand of my brother, from the hand of Esau: for I fear him, lest he will come and smite me, and the mother with the children. And thou saidst, I will surely do thee good, and make thy seed as the sand of the sea, which cannot be numbered for multitude. And he lodged there that same night; and took of that which came to his hand a present for Esau his brother; Two hundred she goats, and twenty he goats, two hundred ewes, and twenty rams, Thirty milch camels with their colts, forty kine, and ten bulls, twenty she asses, and ten foals. And he delivered them into the hand of his servants, every drove by themselves; and said unto his servants, Pass over before me, and put a space betwixt drove and drove. And he commanded the foremost, saying, When Esau my brother meeteth thee, and asketh thee, saying, Whose art thou? and whither goest thou? and whose are these before thee? Then thou shalt say, They be thy servant Jacob's; it is a present sent unto my lord Esau: and, behold, also he is behind us. And so commanded he the second, and the third, and all that followed the droves, saying, On this manner shall ye speak unto Esau, when ye find him. And say ye moreover, Behold, thy servant Jacob is behind us. For he said, I will appease him with the present that goeth before me, and afterward I will see his face; peradventure he will accept of me. So went the present over before him: and himself lodged that night in the company. And he rose up that night, and took his two wives, and his two womenservants, and his eleven sons, and passed over the ford Jabbok. And he took them, and sent them over the brook, and sent over that he had.

Jacob Wrestles With an Angel

And Jacob was left alone; and there came a man at eventide who was naked, and set well in his strength. Now the face of the man was held in shade; and that man did set upon Jacob with his hands and his legs. And the man and Jacob strove against each other. And the man did twist the arms of Jacob. And Jacob did slip from his grasp, and made a bind upon the man with his legs. And the man was above Jacob; and Jacob was below. And the man struck with hands; and Jacob struck with fists. And the man grasped the hair of Jacob, and kissed him as they strove against each to each. But Jacob was sly, and kissed the man as a woman would, and then wrestled still against the man well set in his strength, and whose face remained in the shade. And Jacob and the man moved betwixt wrestling, and setting upon the thighs of the other with hand and with mouth. In darkness were Jacob and the man covered in the dust of the ground, and the sweat of the brow. And they wrestled all through the night: seeming without end. And Jacob and the man strove until the precious time when the breaking of the day comes. And when the man saw that he prevailed not against him, he touched the hollow of the thigh of Jacob betwixt the jewels of Jacob and his secret; and the hollow of Jacob's thigh was out of joint, as he wrestled with him. And the man said, Let me go, for the day breaketh. And Jacob said, I will not let thee go, except thou bless me. And the man said unto him, What is thy name? And he said, Jacob. And the man said, Thy name shall be called no more Jacob, but Israel: for as a prince hast thou power with God and with men, and hast prevailed. And Jacob asked him, and said, Tell me, I pray thee, thy name. And the man said, Wherefore is it that thou dost ask after my name? And he blessed him there. And Jacob called the name of the place Peniel: for I have seen God face to face, and my life is preserved. And as he passed over Penuel the sun rose upon him, and he halted upon his thigh. Therefore the children of Israel eat not of the sinew which shrank, which is upon the hollow of the thigh, unto this day: because he touched the hollow of Jacob's thigh in the sinew that shrank.

Jacob and Esau Reconciled

nd Jacob lifted up his eyes, and looked, and, behold, Esau came, and with him four hundred men. And he divided the children unto Leah, and unto Rachel, and unto the two handmaids. And he put the handmaids and their children foremost, and Leah and her children after, and Rachel and Joseph hindermost. And he passed over before them, and bowed himself to the ground seven times, until he came near to his brother. And Esau ran to meet him, and embraced him, and fell on his neck, and kissed him: and they wept. And he lifted up his eyes, and saw the women and the children; and said, Who are those with thee? And he said, The children which God hath graciously given thy servant. Then the handmaidens came near, they and their children, and they bowed themselves. And Leah also with her children came near, and bowed themselves: and after came Joseph near and Rachel, and they bowed themselves. And he said, What meanest thou by all this drove which I met? And he said, These are to find grace in the sight of my lord. And Esau said, I have enough, my brother; keep that thou hast unto thyself. And Jacob said, Nay, I pray thee, if now I have found grace in thy sight, then receive my present at my hand: for therefore I have seen thy face, as though I had seen the face of God, and thou wast pleased with me. Take, I pray thee, my blessing that is brought to thee; because God hath dealt graciously with me, and because I have enough. And he urged him, and he took it. And he said, Let us take our journey, and let us go, and I will go before thee. And he said unto him, My lord knoweth that the children are tender, and the flocks and herds with young are with me: and if men should overdrive them one day, all the flock will die. Let my lord, I pray thee, pass over before his servant: and I will lead on softly, according as the cattle that goeth before me and the children be able to endure, until I come unto my lord unto Seir. And Esau said, Let me now leave with thee some of the folk that are with me. And he said, What needeth it? let me find grace in the sight of my lord.

So Esau returned that day on his way unto Seir. And Jacob journeyed to Succoth, and built him an house, and made booths for his cattle: therefore the name of the place is called Succoth. And Jacob came to Shalem, a city of Shechem, which is in the land of Canaan, when he came from Padan-aram; and pitched his tent before the city. And he bought a parcel of a field, where he had spread his tent, at the hand of the children of Hamor, Shechem's father, for an hundred pieces of money. And he erected there an altar, and called it El-elohe-Israel.

The Taking of Dinah

nd Dinah the daughter of Leah, which she bare unto Jacob, went out to see the daughters of the land. And when Shechem the son of Hamor the Hivite, prince of the country, saw her, he took her without cause or reason to the heart of man, and forgot all customs. And Shechem knew not that Esau and Jacob were welcome in the land. And Dinah did struggle and strive against Shechem. And she did raise her hands to him, and struck him in the hollow of his thigh by her heel. And yet he lay with her, and he defiled her with cruel roughness upon her breast and her secrets beneath her skins. And his soul clave unto Dinah the daughter of Jacob, and he loved the damsel, and spake kindly unto the damsel after his deed was done. And Shechem spake unto his father Hamor, saying, Get me this damsel to wife. And Jacob heard that Shechem had defiled Dinah his daughter: now his sons were with his cattle in the field: and Jacob held his peace until they were come.

And Hamor the father of Shechem went out unto Jacob to commune with him. And the sons of Jacob came out of the field when they heard it: and the men were grieved, and they were very wroth, because he had wrought folly in Israel in lying with Jacob's daughter; which thing ought not to be done. And Hamor communed with them, saying, The soul of my son Shechem longeth for your daughter: I pray you give her him to wife. And make ye marriages with us, and give your daughters unto us, and take our daughters unto you. And ye shall dwell with us: and the land shall be before you; dwell and trade ye therein, and get you possessions therein. And Shechem said unto her father, Jacob and unto her brethren, Let me find grace in your eyes and make right that which I have wronged and cleve to her in devotion, and what ye shall say unto me I will give. Ask me never so much dowry and gift, and I will give according as ye shall say unto me: but give me the damsel to wife. And the sons of Jacob answered Shechem and Hamor his father deceitfully, and said, because he had defiled Dinah their sister: And they said unto them, We cannot do this thing, to give our sister to one that is uncircumcised; for that were a reproach unto us: But in this will we consent unto you: If ye will be as we be, that every male of you be circumcised; Then will we give our daughters unto you, and we will take your daughters to us, and we will dwell with you, and we will become one people. But if ye will not hearken unto us, to be circumcised; then will we take our daughter, and we will be gone. And their words pleased Hamor, and Shechem Hamor's son. And the young man deferred not to do the thing, because he had delight in Jacob's daughter: and he was more honourable than all the house of his father.

And Hamor and Shechem his son came unto the gate of their city, and communed with the men of their city, saying, These men are peaceable with us; therefore let them dwell in the land, and trade therein; for the land, behold, it is large enough for them; let us take their daughters to us for wives, and let us give them our daughters. Only herein will the men consent unto us for to dwell with us, to be one people, if every male among us be circumcised, as they are circumcised. Shall not their cattle and their substance and every beast of theirs be ours? only let us consent unto them, and they will dwell with us. And unto Hamor and unto Shechem his son hearkened all that went out of the gate of his city; and every male was circumcised, all that went out of the gate of his city.

And it came to pass on the third day when the men of Shalem were sore and still confined to bed, that two of the sons of Jacob, Simeon and Levi, Dinah's brethren, cloaked themselves in the night. They crept unto Dinah in the tent whence she was kept bound and asked her, What wouldest thou have us do to the men of Shalem who are now sore, and confined to their beds? And Dinah said, For my maidenhead is stolen; and my honour is gone from my Father and my brethren. I strove with one, and ate of a dish of pain. Hence I have lost all but my life; may it not be so again. I pray thee to take theirs.

And it was before the sun did arise, while the men of Shalem were sore and still in bed, that these two sons of Jacob, Simeon and Levi, Dinah's brethren, took each man to his sword, and came upon the city boldly, and slew all the males. And they slew Hamor and Shechem his son with the edge of the sword, and took Dinah out of Shechem's house, and went out. The sons of Jacob came upon the slain, and spoiled the city, because they had defiled their sister. They took their sheep, and their oxen, and their asses, and that which was in the city, and that which was in the field, And all their wealth, and all their little ones, and their wives took they captive, and spoiled even all that was in the house. And Jacob said to Simeon and Levi, Ye have troubled me to make me to stink among the inhabitants of the land, among the Canaanites and the Perizzites: and I being few in number, they shall gather themselves together against me, and slay me; and I shall be destroyed, I and my house. And they said, Should he deal with our sister as with an harlot?

And God said unto Jacob, Arise, go up to Bethel, and dwell there: and make there an altar unto God, that appeared unto thee when thou fleddest from the face of Esau thy brother. Then Jacob said unto his household, and to all that were with him, Put away the strange gods that are among you, and be clean, and change your garments: And let us arise, and go up to Bethel; and I will make there an altar unto God, who answered me in the day of my distress, and was with me in the way which I went. And they gave unto Jacob all the strange gods which were in their hand, and all their earrings which were in their ears; and Jacob hid them under the oak which was by Shechem. And they journeyed: and the terror of God was upon the cities that were round about them, and they did not pursue after the sons of Jacob.

Jacob Returns to Bethel

o Jacob came to Luz, which is in the land of Canaan, that is, Bethel, he and all the people that were with him. And he built there an altar, and called the place El-beth-el: because there God appeared unto him, when he fled from the face of his brother. But Deborah Rebekah's nurse died, and she was buried beneath Bethel under an oak: and the name of it was called Allon-bachuth.

And God appeared unto Jacob again, when he came out of Padan-aram, and blessed him. And God said unto him, Thy name is Jacob: thy name shall not be called any more Jacob, but Israel shall be thy name: and he called his name Israel. And God said unto him, I am God Almighty: be fruitful and multiply; a nation and a company of nations shall be of thee, and kings shall come out of thy loins; And the land which I gave Abraham and Isaac, to thee I will give it, and to thy seed after thee will I give the land. And God went up from him in the place where he talked with him. And Jacob set up a pillar in the place where he talked with him, even a pillar of stone: and he poured a drink offering thereon, and he poured oil thereon. And Jacob called the name of the place where God spake with him, Bethel.

And they journeyed from Bethel; and there was but a little way to come to Ephrath: And in the night when the moon was high, Jacob came upon his dearest love Rachel; and he recounted of the well whereon he did spy her. And Rachel did laugh with the story of Jacob uncovering the well for the watering of the sheep. And Jacob did uncover the well of Rachel that night, and was watered. And Rachel nursed the halt in his thigh with her mouth, and held him fast betwixt her legs. And she conceived whilst in his arms.

And Rachel travailed, and she had hard labour. And it came to pass, when she was in hard labour, that the midwife said unto her, Fear not; thou shalt have this son also. And it came to pass, as her soul was in departing, (for she died) that she called his name Ben-oni: but his father called him Benjamin. And Rachel died, and was buried in the way to Ephrath, which is Bethlehem. And Jacob set a pillar that bore the image of blossoms at its heavenmost end upon her grave: the grave that was in the very earth. That is the pillar of Rachel's grave unto this day that stands to mark the pillar of Israel in its home above the field of Rachel.

And Israel journeyed, and spread his tent beyond the tower of Edar and bedded with Bilhah. And it came to pass that great wroth rose in Reuben upon that news. For Reuben said unto himself, Even upon the death of Rachel, still Leah stands behind her in favour. I shall make right of this. I shall give place to a mother most honoured and goodly. Goodly to Jacob, despite his scorn, and goodly to LORD. Now she may learn of all the secrets that the LORD has spoken unto Israel.

And it came to pass when Israel dwelt in that land, that Reuben, the son of Leah went and shaved his face, and arms, and made himself a smooth man like his father Jacob. And Reuben lay with Bilhah his father's concubine Rachel's maid. And it was on a night when no moon was in the heavens. Reuben said unto Bilhah, Woman I come and claim you for loving this very night. And Bilhah took his hands, and clasped his face and said, Thy voice is Reuben's yet thy hands and face are those of Jacob. And Reuben said, Bilhah indeed, I am Israel. Feel me and know that. And Bilhah did take on the visitor with gladness to her tent, believing it was Israel coming upon her again. But it was not Israel at her thighs, and breast, and mouth. It was but Reuben, the fruit of the womb of Leah, who knew the secrets of Bilhah that night. And Bilhah trembled in delight at his hands, and then freed her halting words to shew her delight in the man at her thighs. And he said, I have hastened unto to thee; for thou art with great beauty. And with her words shewn, and his words shewn, she shewed her secrets; and upon her skins and her breast did Reuben press upon. And they became of one tongue; and their wool became of one wool.

And when the threshold of day did come and light broke, Reuben said unto Bilhah, Behold Bilhah, I am not my father Israel; I am but Reuben in his place. I cast upon the name of my father; for now thou hast taken favour in his eyes and, lo, still Leah has none from Jacob. Now the rank of Leah shall rise.

And Bilhah fled in fear and sorrow from the deception at her heel. And Israel heard it be told and stripped Reuben of his birthright and never wifed Bilhah again.

Now the sons of Jacob were twelve: The sons of Leah; Reuben, Jacob's firstborn, and Simeon, and Levi, and Judah, and Issachar, and Zebulun: The sons of Rachel; Joseph, and

Benjamin: And the sons of Bilhah, Rachel's handmaid; Dan, and Naphtali: And the sons of Zilpah, Leah's handmaid; Gad, and Asher: these are the sons of Jacob, which were born to him in Padan-aram.

And Jacob came unto Isaac his father unto Mamre, unto the city of Arbah, which is Hebron, where Abraham and Isaac sojourned. And the days of Isaac were an hundred and fourscore years. And Isaac gave up the ghost, and died, and was gathered unto his people, being old and full of days: and his sons Esau and Jacob buried him.

The Descendants of Esau

ow these are the generations of Esau, who is Edom. Esau took his wives of the daughters of Canaan; Adah the daughter of Elon the Hittite, and Aholibamah the daughter of Anah the daughter of Zibeon the Hivite; And Bashemath Ishmael's daughter, sister of Nebajoth. And Adah bare to Esau Eliphaz; and Bashemath bare Reuel; And Aholibamah bare Jeush, and Jaalam, and Korah: these are the sons of Esau, which were born unto him in the land of Canaan.

And Esau took his wives, and his sons, and his daughters, and all the persons of his house, and his cattle, and all his beasts, and all his substance, which he had got in the land of Canaan; and went into the country from the face of his brother Jacob. For their riches were more than that they might dwell together; and the land wherein they were strangers could not bear them because of their cattle. Thus dwelt Esau in mount Seir: Esau is Edom.

And these are the generations of Esau the father of the Edomites in mount Seir: These are the names of Esau's sons; Eliphaz the son of Adah the wife of Esau, Reuel the son of Bashemath the wife of Esau. And the sons of Eliphaz were Teman, Omar, Zepho, and Gatam, and Kenaz. And Timna was concubine to Eliphaz Esau's son; and she bare to Eliphaz

Amalek: these were the sons of Adah Esau's wife. And these are the sons of Reuel; Nahath, and Zerah, Shammah, and Mizzah: these were the sons of Bashemath Esau's wife. And these were the sons of Aholibamah, the daughter of Anah the daughter of Zibeon, Esau's wife: and she bare to Esau Jeush, and Jaalam, and Korah.

These were dukes of the sons of Esau: the sons of Eliphaz the firstborn son of Esau; duke Teman, duke Omar, duke Zepho, duke Kenaz, Duke Korah, duke Gatam, and duke Amalek: these are the dukes that came of Eliphaz in the land of Edom; these were the sons of Adah.

And these are the sons of Reuel Esau's son; duke Nahath, duke Zerah, duke Shammah, duke Mizzah: these are the dukes that came of Reuel in the land of Edom; these are the sons of Bashemath Esau's wife. And these are the sons of Aholibamah Esau's wife; duke Jeush, duke Jaalam, duke Korah: these were the dukes that came of Aholibamah the daughter of Anah, Esau's wife. These are the sons of Esau, who is Edom, and these are their dukes.

These are the sons of Seir the Horite, who inhabited the land; Lotan, and Shobal, and Zibeon, and Anah, And Dishon, and Ezer, and Dishan: these are the dukes of the Horites, the children of Seir in the land of Edom. And the children of Lotan were Hori and Hemam; and Lotan's sister was Timna. And the children of Shobal were these; Alvan, and Manahath, and Ebal, Shepho, and Onam. And these are the children of Zibeon; both Ajah, and Anah: this was that Anah that found the mules in the wilderness, as he fed the asses of Zibeon his father. And the children of Anah were these; Dishon, and Aholibamah the daughter of Anah. And these are the children of Dishon; Hemdan, and Eshban, and Ithran, and Cheran. The children of Ezer are these; Bilhan, and Zaavan, and Akan. The children of Dishan are these; Uz, and Aran. These are the dukes that came of the Horites; duke Lotan, duke Shobal, duke Zibeon, duke Anah, Duke Dishon, duke Ezer, duke Dishan: these are the dukes that came of Hori, among their dukes in the land of Seir.

And these are the kings that reigned in the land of Edom, before there reigned any king over the children of Israel. And Bela the son of Beor reigned in Edom: and the name of his city was Dinhabah. And Bela died, and Jobab the son of Zerah of Bozrah reigned in his stead. And Jobab died, and Husham of the land of Temani reigned in his stead. And Husham died, and Hadad the son of Bedad, who smote Midian in the field of Moab, reigned in his stead: and the name of his city was Avith. And Hadad died, and Samlah of Masrekah reigned in his stead. And Samlah died, and Saul of Rehoboth by the river reigned in his stead. And Saul died, and Baal-hanan the son of Achbor reigned in his stead. And Baal-hanan the son of Achbor died, and Hadar reigned in his stead: and the name of his city was Pau; and his wife's name was Mehetabel, the daughter of Matred, the daughter of Mezahab.

Hadar ruled by the day; and in the nights Mehetabel ruled over him. For Hadar grew weary of ruling; and it weighed heavy upon his brow. And Mehetabel took his staff and crown, and commanded him to lay still. And she entreated him in his hapless state to kneel before her, and submit to her audits, and beg to sup at her thighs. And when his begging was not to the liking of Mehetabel, she struck him with his staff upon his arms, and upon his back. And when he did please her, she crowned his labours and kissed the marks that she left; and he gave thanks to Mehetabel, and knew the garden untouched by her breast. And Hadar ruled well, and feared not to shew his marks as a sign of his strength.

And these are the names of the dukes that came of Esau, according to their families, after their places, by their names; duke Timnah, duke Alvah, duke Jetheth, Duke Aholibamah, duke Elah, duke Pinon, Duke Kenaz, duke Teman, duke Mibzar, Duke Magdiel, duke Iram: these be the dukes of Edom, according to their habitations in the land of their possession: he is Esau the father of the Edomites.

Joseph and His Brothers

nd Jacob dwelt in the land wherein his father was a stranger, in the land of Canaan. These are the generations of Jacob. Joseph, being seventeen years old, was feeding the flock with his brethren; and the lad was with the sons of Bilhah, and with the sons of Zilpah, his father's wives: and Joseph brought unto his father their evil report. Now Israel loved Joseph more than all his children, because he was the son of his old age and the son of Rachel, his beloved: and he made him a coat of many colours. And when his brethren saw that their father loved him more than all his brethren, they hated him, and could not speak peaceably unto him.

And Joseph dreamed a dream, and he told it his brethren: and they hated him yet the more. And he said unto them, Hear, I pray you, this dream which I have dreamed: For, behold, we were binding sheaves in the field, and, lo, my sheaf arose, and also stood upright, long and fat; and, behold, your sheaves, short and thin, stood round about, and made obeisance to my sheaf. And his brethren said to him, Shalt thou indeed reign over us? Or shalt thou indeed have dominion over us? Shall thy sheaf be used upon man or woman; or only shall it feed thy hand? And they hated him yet the more for his dreams, and for his words.

And he dreamed yet another dream, and told it his brethren, and said, Behold, I have dreamed a dream more; and, behold, the sun and the moon and the eleven stars made obeisance to me. And he told it to his father, and to his brethren: and his father rebuked him, and said unto him, What is this dream that thou hast dreamed? Shall I and thy mother and thy brethren indeed come to bow down ourselves to thee to the earth? And his brethren envied him; but his father observed the saying.

And his brethren went to feed their father's flock in Shechem. And Israel said unto Joseph, Do not thy brethren feed the flock in Shechem? come, and I will send thee unto them. And he said to him, Here am I. And he said to him, Go, I pray thee, see whether it be well with thy brethren, and well with the flocks; and bring me word again. So he sent him out of the vale of Hebron, and he came to Shechem.

And a certain man found him, and, behold, he was wandering in the field: and the man asked him, saying, What seekest thou? And he said, I seek my brethren: tell me, I pray thee, where they feed their flocks. And the man said, They are departed hence; for I heard them say, Let us go to Dothan. And Joseph went after his brethren, and found them in Dothan. And when they saw him afar off, even before he came near unto them, they conspired against him to slay him. And they said one to another, Behold, this dreamer cometh. Come now therefore, and let us slay him, and cast him into some pit, and we will say, Some evil beast hath devoured him: and we shall see what will become of his dreams. And Reuben heard it, and he delivered him out of their hands; and said, Let us not kill him. And Reuben said unto them, Shed no blood, but cast him into this pit that is in the wilderness, and lay no hand upon him; that he might rid him out of their hands, to deliver him to his father again.

And it came to pass, when Joseph was come unto his brethren, that they stript Joseph out of his coat, his coat of many colours that was on him; And they took him, and cast him into a pit: and the pit was empty, there was no water in it. And Gad said, Lo, thy sheaf is small, now that we see it. And Joseph was afraid. Joseph called out to his brethren. And he begged upon his brethren his sorriness for being a proud fool. And the sons of Leah, and Bilhah, and Zilpah did cover their ears. And they sat down to eat bread: and they lifted up their eyes and looked, and, behold, a company of Ishmeelites came from Gilead with their camels bearing spicery and balm and myrrh, going to carry it down to Egypt. And Judah said unto his brethren, What profit is it if we slay our brother, and conceal his blood? Come, and let us sell him to the Ishmeelites, and let not our hand be upon him; for he is our brother and our flesh. And his brethren were content. Then there passed by Midianites merchantmen; and they saw that the face of Joseph was fair and drew and lifted up Joseph out of the pit, and sold Joseph to the Ishmeelites for twenty pieces of silver: and they brought Joseph into Egypt.

And Reuben returned unto the pit; and, behold, Joseph was not in the pit; and he rent his clothes. And he returned unto his brethren, and said, The child is not; and I, whither shall I go? And they took Joseph's coat, and killed a kid of the goats, and dipped the coat in the blood; And they sent the coat of many colours, and they brought it to their father; and said, This have we found: know now whether it be thy son's coat or no. And he knew it, and said, It is my son's coat; an evil beast hath devoured him; Joseph is without doubt rent in pieces. And Jacob rent his clothes, and put sackcloth upon his loins, and mourned for his son many days. And all his sons and all his daughters rose up to comfort him; but he refused to be comforted; and he said, For I will go down into the grave unto my son mourning. Thus his father wept for him. And the Midianites sold him into Egypt unto Potiphar, an officer of Pharaoh's, and captain of the guard.

Judah and Tamar

And it came to pass at that time, that Judah went down from his brethren, and turned in to a certain Adullamite, whose name was Hirah. And Judah saw there a daughter of a certain Canaanite, whose name was Shuah, and the name of the daughter was Aliyath. Now Aliyath was fair in name and face; and her hair shone bright. And all men longed to touch upon her hair, and to smooth it yet more. And, yea, Judah took her, and went in unto her with gladness. And her skirts were lifted, and her nakedness exposed unto his feet. And her nakedness was entered; and her seed knew the seed of Judah. And she conceived, and bare a son; and he called his name Er. And Aliyath longed for another son; so in the night she came unto Judah, and draped her hair across the staff of Judah, and awoke the staff. And with great joy was he awakened to the smoothness of her hair upon him. And she took the staff, and kept it within her folds. And from his staff came a great oil that came into and was mixed with the waters of Aliyath. Then she conceived again, and bare a son; and she called his name Onan. Then in the day she came unto Judah in the fields, away from the other men, and she bowed to the staff of Judah and kissed it. And the staff did rule over the lands of Aliyath, where a fire did burn that yearned to be slaked. And he did plow those lands, and seeded them; and he did drink of the waters that he ruled. And she yet again conceived, and bare a son; and called his name Shelah: and he was at Chezib, when she bare him.

And Judah took a wife for Er his firstborn, whose name was Tamar. And Er, Judah's firstborn, was wicked in the sight of the LORD; and the LORD slew him. And Judah said unto Onan, Go in unto thy brother's wife, and marry her, and raise up seed to thy brother as is the custom to which is right. And Onan knew that the seed should not be his; and it came to pass, when he went in unto his brother's wife Tamar, that Onan kissed upon her and held her. And Tamar did hunger for child, and for knowing. And Tamar readied the staff of Onan by her hand, and by her secrets. And Onan did know her in her smoothness. But as the time came, he withdrew that there, and he spilled it upon the ground, lest that he should give seed to his brother. And the thing which he did displeased the LORD: wherefore he slew him also; for the custom was to make the brother give seed for his brother. Then said Judah to Tamar his daughter in law, Remain a widow at thy father's house, till Shelah my son be grown: for he said, Lest peradventure he die also, as his brethren did. And Tamar went and dwelt in her father's house.

And in process of time the daughter of Shuah, Aliyath, Judah's wife died; and Judah was comforted, and went up unto his sheepshearers to Timnath, he and his friend Hirah the Adullamite. And it was told Tamar, saying, Behold thy father in law goeth up to Timnath to shear his sheep. And she put her widow's garments off from her, and covered her with a vail, and wrapped herself, and sat in an open place, which is by the way to Timnath; for she saw that Shelah was grown, and she was not given unto him to wife. When Judah saw her, he thought her to be an harlot; because she had covered her face. And he turned unto her by the way, and said, Go to, I pray thee, let me come in unto thee; (for he knew not that she was his daughter in law.) And she said, What wilt thou give me, that thou mayest come in unto me? And he said, I will send thee a kid from the flock. And she said, Wilt thou give me a pledge, till thou send it? And he said, What pledge shall I give thee? And she said, Thy signet, and thy bracelets, and thy staff that is in thine hand. And he gave her the signet and bracelets. And he also gave the staff to her. And Tamar asked, What of thy staff that is secret to thee, and amongst thy skins? And he said, If that is the pledge thou seekest, then thou shouldest unravel it. And she took the staff within her secrets as she bent upon a rock. And the staff hid within her mouth as her face remained covered with that vail. And she knew the strength in his thighs. And Judah drank of her waters, and brought them both to the garden. Then he scattered his seed within her womb, and came in unto her twice; and she conceived by him. And she arose, and went away, and laid by her vail from her, and put on the garments of her widowhood.

And Judah sent the kid by the hand of his friend the Adullamite, to receive his pledge from the woman's hand: but he found her not. Then he asked the men of that place, saying, Where is the harlot, that was openly by the way side? And they said, There was no harlot in this place. And he returned to Judah, and said, I cannot find her; and also the men of the place said, that there was no harlot in this place. And Judah said, Let her take it to her, lest we be shamed: behold, I sent this kid, and thou hast not found her.

And it came to pass about three months after, that it was told Judah, saying, Tamar thy daughter in law hath played the harlot; and also, behold, she is with child by whoredom. And Judah said, Bring her forth, and let her be burnt. When she was brought forth, she sent to her father in law, saying, By the man, whose these are, am I with child: and she said, Discern, I pray thee, whose are these, the signet and bracelets, and staff? And Judah acknowledged them, and said, She hath been more righteous than I; because that I gave her not to Shelah my son. And he knew her again no more.

And it came to pass in the time of her travail, that, behold, twins were in her womb. And it came to pass, when she travailed, that the one put out his hand: and the midwife took and bound upon his hand a scarlet thread, saying, This came out first, And it came to pass, as he drew back his hand, that, behold, his brother came out: and she said, How hast thou broken forth? this breach be upon thee: therefore his name was called Pharez. And afterward came out his brother, that had the scarlet thread upon his hand: and his name was called Zarah.

Joseph, Potiphar and Potiphar's Wife

And Joseph was brought down to Egypt; and Potiphar, an officer of Pharaoh, captain of the guard, an Egyptian, bought him of the hands of the Ishmeelites, which had brought him down thither. And the LORD was with Joseph, and he was a prosperous man; and he was in the house of his master the Egyptian Potiphar. And his master saw that the LORD was with him, and that the LORD made all that he did to prosper in his hand. And Joseph found grace in his sight; for Joseph walked with swaying hips; and he served him in all ways. And Potiphar came in unto Joseph; for he was tempted by his fair graces. And he lifted his skirt, and gave himself delight in the halls of Joseph. And Joseph kneeled with pleasure unto his master. And he tended unto the spear of his master, and gave wise counsel with his mouth late into the night. And in the long days with guardsmen, Potiphar did come into his home to be tended by the ministrations of Joseph upon him. And Potiphar did call upon magicians, who, by oils and castings, did enlarge the sheaf of Joseph for the sake of him. And Potiphar made him overseer over his house, and all that he had he put into his hand. And it came to pass from the time that he had made him overseer in his house, and over all that he had, that the LORD blessed the Egyptian's house for Joseph's sake; and the blessing of the LORD was upon all that he had in the house, and in the field. And he left all that he had in Joseph's hand; and he knew not ought he had, save the bread which he did eat. And Joseph was a goodly person, and well favoured.

And the wife of Potiphar was called Zelicah. And her mind was drawn to the fairness of the countenance of Joseph; and she spake of him unto her sisters in the court of the king of Egypt. And they mocked her. For thou find favour in an Hebrew and mere slave? Yea, how can it be so? And Zelicah called unto them to visit her in her house to be tested. And Zelicah said unto the lot of them, Take these fruits, and wield these knives to cut them asunder. And as they took the fruit to their purpose, Zelicah called unto Joseph to come and serve her. And Joseph did come. And when the lot of women did see the beauteous Joseph, each of their hands did slip; and their knives drew blood from their hands. And when the room was clear of Joseph, the lot of women fell to their knees at the feet of Zelicah and said, Pitiful are we for doubting thee. Forgive us for thy slave is more fair than any other; and our ardour is raised in our thighs, and upon our breasts. And Zelicah said, Gratitude for thy atonements unto me. Ye have only seen him for but one moment. For he lives here; and I witness him each day, and hear his wise voice, and see his fair face. He as an ember unto me in my hearth. I long to worship at the altar of Joseph.

And it came to pass after these things, that his master's wife, Zelicah, cast her eyes upon fair Joseph; and she said, Lie with me. But he refused, and said unto his master's wife, For I am just a boy unto the man that is Potiphar my master. I cannot give what you ask; for it is not mine to give. I am of Potiphar alone. And if he wills it unto me to come in unto you, lo, I shall do it. Behold, my master wotteth not what is with me in the house, and he hath committed all that he hath to my hand; There is none greater in this house than I; neither hath he kept back any thing from me but thee, because thou art his wife: how then can I do this great wickedness, and sin against God?

And it came to pass, as she spake to Joseph day by day, that he hearkened not unto her, to lie by her, or to be with her. And it came to pass about this time, that Joseph went into the house to do his business; and there was none of the men of the house there within. And Zelicah caught him by his garment, saying, Lie with me; and shew me why Potiphar adores thee so. Shew unto me thy new sheaf, and thy ministrations by thy hand, and mouth, and back: and he left his garment in her hand, and fled in nakedness, and got him out. And Zelicah was wroth; and the tree of spite flowered in her breast. For if she could not have Joseph, none would. And it came to pass, when she saw that he had left his garment in her hand, and was fled forth, That she called unto the men of her house, and spake unto them, saying, See, he hath brought in an Hebrew unto us to mock us; he came in unto me to lie with me, and I cried with a loud voice: And it came to pass, when he heard that I lifted up my voice and cried, that he left his garment with me, and fled, and got him out. And she laid up his garment by her, until his lord came home. And she spake unto him according to these words, saying, The Hebrew servant, which thou hast brought unto us, came in unto me to defile and mock me: And it came to pass, as I lifted up my voice and cried, that he left his garment with me, and fled out. And it came to pass, when his master heard the words of Zelicah, which she spake unto him, saying, After this manner did thy servant to me; that his wrath was kindled. And Joseph's master took him, and put him into the prison, a place where the king's prisoners were bound: and he was there in the prison.

Joseph Interprets
Dreams in Prison

ut the LORD was with Joseph, and shewed him mercy, and gave him favour in the sight of the keeper of the prison. And the keeper of the prison committed to Joseph's hand all the prisoners that were in the prison. And he bowed to tend to the heel of Joseph each night; for he saw the lament in the heart of Joseph for all he had lost. And the wounded heart of Joseph was tended as his heel was bowed down to. And whatsoever they did there, he was the doer of it. The keeper of the prison looked not to any thing that was under his hand; because the LORD was with him, and that which he did, the LORD made it to prosper.

And it came to pass after these things, that the butler of the king of Egypt and his baker had offended their lord the king of Egypt. And Pharaoh was wroth against two of his officers, against the chief of the butlers, and against the chief of the bakers. And he put them in ward in the house of the captain of the guard, into the prison, the place where Joseph was bound. And the captain of the guard charged Joseph with them, and he served them: and they continued a season in ward.

Now the chief of the butlers and the chief of the bakers each knew the other man from their years in the court of the king of Egypt, and did not stain their youthful years in avarice. Nor were the two men known as tongue and teeth to the other. So finding themselves exiled to ward thusly, they became as arrow and quiver to the other. For none knew the court as they had known it. And they wept as they spake of broken cisterns and stones, and clasped each other for comforts. And strife was the day at the ward amongst the bandits and thieves. But peace was the night when the baker oiled the quiver of the butler, and put but barbs of love into it. And they pressed breast to back, and came to rest side to side. And they dreamed a dream both of them, each man his dream in one night, each man according to the interpretation of his dream, the butler and the baker of the king of Egypt, which were bound in the prison. And Joseph came in unto them in the morning, and looked upon them, and, behold, they were sad. And he asked Pharaoh's officers that were with him in the ward of his lord's house, saying, Wherefore look ye so sadly to day? And they said unto him, We have dreamed a dream, and there is no interpreter of it. And Joseph said unto them, Do not interpretations belong to God? tell me them, I pray you. And the chief butler told his dream to Joseph, and said to him, In my dream, behold, a vine was before me; And in the vine were three branches: and it was as though it budded, and her blossoms shot forth; and the clusters thereof brought forth ripe grapes: And Pharaoh's cup was in my hand: and I took the grapes, and pressed them into Pharaoh's cup, and I gave the cup into Pharaoh's hand.

And Joseph said unto him, This is the interpretation of it: The three branches are three days: Yet within three days shall Pharaoh lift up thine head, and restore thee unto thy place: and thou shalt deliver Pharaoh's cup into his hand, after the former manner when thou wast his butler. But think on me when it shall be well with thee, and shew kindness, I pray thee, unto me, and make mention of me unto Pharaoh, and bring me out of this house: For indeed I was stolen away out of the land of the Hebrews: and here also have I done nothing that they should put me into the dungeon.

When the chief baker saw that the interpretation was good, he said unto Joseph, I also was in my dream, and, behold, I had three white baskets on my head: And in the uppermost basket there was of all manner of bakemeats for Pharaoh; and the birds did eat them out of the basket upon my head. And Joseph answered and said, This is the interpretation thereof: The three baskets are three days: Yet within three days shall Pharaoh lift up thy head from off thee, and shall hang thee on a tree; and the birds shall eat thy flesh from off thee.

And the baker shook in fear, and said, Joseph thy words are piercings unto my ears. Hast thou but a dream now of a second meaning? I am unstrung. And surely I shall die. And the butler held fast unto the baker, and whispered unto him to fear not. But the baker said unto the butler, Nay, we are as two brooks running apart, then joining, then dividing again. And your stream runs on. And mine but ends, brittle and dry.

And it came to pass the third day, which was Pharaoh's birthday, that he made a feast unto all his servants: and he lifted up the head of the chief butler and of the chief baker among his servants. And he restored the chief butler unto his butlership again; and he gave the cup into Pharaoh's hand: But he hanged the chief baker: as Joseph had interpreted to them. Yet did not the chief butler remember Joseph, but forgat him.

Joseph Interprets Pharaoh's Dreams

And it came to pass at the end of two full years, that Pharaoh dreamed: and, behold, he stood by the river. And, behold, there came up out of the river seven well favoured kine and fatfleshed; and they fed in a meadow. And, behold, seven other kine came up after them out of the river, ill favoured and leanfleshed; and stood by the other kine upon the brink of the river. And the ill favoured and leanfleshed kine did eat up the seven well favoured and fat kine. So Pharaoh awoke. And he slept and dreamed the second time: and, behold, seven ears of corn came up upon one stalk, rank and good. And, behold, seven thin ears and blasted with the east wind sprung up after them. And the seven thin ears devoured the seven rank and full ears. And Pharaoh awoke, and, behold, it was a dream. And it came to pass in the morning that his spirit was troubled; and he sent and called for all the magicians of Egypt, and all the wise men thereof: and Pharaoh told them his dream; but there was none that could interpret them unto Pharaoh.

Then spake the chief butler unto Pharaoh, saying, I do remember my faults this day: Pharaoh was wroth with his servants, and put me in ward in the captain of the guard's house, both me and the chief baker: And we dreamed a dream in one night, I and he; we dreamed each man according to the interpretation of his dream. And there was there with us a young man, an Hebrew, servant to the captain of the guard; and we told him, and he interpreted to us our dreams; to each man according to his dream he did interpret. And it came to pass, as he interpreted to us, so it was; me he restored unto mine office, and him he hanged.

Then Pharaoh sent and called Joseph, and they brought him hastily out of the dungeon: and he shaved himself, and changed his raiment, and came in unto Pharaoh. And Pharaoh said unto Joseph, I have dreamed a dream, and there is none that can interpret it: and I have heard say of thee, that thou canst understand a dream to interpret it. And Joseph answered Pharaoh, saying, It is not in me: God shall give Pharaoh an answer of peace. And Pharaoh said unto Joseph, In my dream, behold, I stood upon the bank of the river: And, behold, there came up out of the river seven kine, fatfleshed and well favoured; and they fed in a meadow: And, behold, seven other kine came up after them, poor and very ill favoured and leanfleshed, such as I never saw in all the land of Egypt for badness: And the lean and the ill favoured kine did eat up the first seven fat kine: And when they had eaten them up, it could not be known that they had eaten them; but they were still ill favoured, as at the beginning. So I awoke. And I saw in my dream, and, behold, seven ears came up in one stalk, full and good: And, behold, seven ears, withered, thin, and blasted with the east wind, sprung up after them: And the thin ears devoured the seven good ears: and I told this unto the magicians; but there was none that could declare it to me.

And Joseph said unto Pharaoh, The dream of Pharaoh is one: God hath shewed Pharaoh what he is about to do. The seven good kine are seven years; and the seven good ears are seven years: the dream is one. And the seven thin and ill favoured kine that came up after them are seven years; and the seven empty ears blasted with the east wind shall be seven years of famine. This is the thing which I have spoken unto Pharaoh: What God is about to do he sheweth unto Pharaoh. Behold, there come seven years of great plenty throughout all the land of Egypt: And there shall arise after them seven years of famine; and all the plenty shall be forgotten in the land of Egypt; and the famine shall consume the land; And the plenty shall not be known in the land by reason of that famine following; for it shall be very grievous. And for that the dream was doubled unto Pharaoh twice; it is because the thing is established by God, and God will shortly bring it to pass. Now therefore let Pharaoh look out a man discreet and wise, and set him over the land of Egypt. Let Pharaoh do this, and let him appoint officers over the land, and take up the fifth part of the land of Egypt in the seven plenteous years. And let them gather all the food of those good years that come, and lay up corn under the hand of Pharaoh, and let them keep food in the cities. And that food shall be for store to the land against the seven years of famine, which shall be in the land of Egypt; that the land perish not through the famine.

Pharaoh Empowers Joseph

And the thing was good in the eyes of Pharaoh, and in the eyes of all his servants. And Pharaoh said unto his servants, Can we find such a one as this is, a man in whom the Spirit of God is? And Pharaoh said unto Joseph, Forasmuch as God hath shewed thee all this, there is none so discreet and wise as thou art: Thou shalt be over my house, and according unto thy word shall all my people be ruled: only in the throne will I be greater than thou. And Pharaoh said unto Joseph, Thou art both fair and wise. Speak wisdom of thy mouth to my ears, and yet speak with thy mouth to my sceptre that seeds all of Egypt. And Joseph spoke wisely to Pharaoh in his ear, and then kneeled, and spoke with soft tongue to the sceptre of the king of Egypt. Gentle were the palms upon their backs, and long did the oil burn into the night to light their loving. And Pharaoh promised to reward Joseph much for his two wisdoms. Pharaoh said, See, I have set thee over all the rich land of Egypt. And Pharaoh took off his ring from his hand, and put it upon Joseph's hand, and kissed him, and arrayed him in vestures of fine linen in many colours, which Joseph loved. And Pharaoh put a gold chain about the neck of Joseph, and did not pull upon it; And he made him to ride in the second chariot which he had; and they cried before him, Bow the knee: and he made him ruler over all the land of Egypt. And Pharaoh said unto Joseph, I am Pharaoh, and without thee shall no man lift up his hand or foot in all the land of Egypt.

And Pharaoh called Joseph's name Zaphnath-paaneah; and he gave him to wife Asenath the daughter of Poti-pherah priest of On, for that was the custom. And Joseph came in unto her bedding, as was his duty, but he knew not what to do unto her. And Asenath took the hand of Joseph, and placed it to her breast. And he knew it not. And Asenath went to the staff of Joseph; but the staff would not stand. And he knew her not. For the thighs of Asenath confounded him; and her breast vexed him. And they but spurned the sleep as husbands and wives share, but rested apart, as pillars at the gate. And then Joseph went out over all the land of Egypt.

And Joseph was thirty years old when he stood before Pharaoh king of Egypt. And Joseph went out from the presence of Pharaoh, and went throughout all the land of Egypt. And in the seven plenteous years the earth brought forth by handfuls. And he gathered up all the food of the seven years, which were in the land of Egypt, and laid up the food in the cities: the food of the field, which was round about every city, laid he up in the same. And Joseph gathered corn as the sand of the sea, very much, until he left numbering; for it was without number. And with the corn, Joseph also gathered new wisdom of the ways of women from deep in every corner of Egypt; for the women of Egypt had kept all the secrets of knowing wisely. And he took that wisdom in unto Asenath, when he returned. And he brought Asenath to great heights of joys by his hand and by his mouth. And the staff of Joseph stood in the country of Asenath. And, lo, the job was done for its sake alone, and for the joy of Asenath, and not his own. And unto Joseph were born two sons, as was the custom, before the years of famine came, which Asenath the daughter of Poti- pherah priest of On bare unto him. And Joseph called the name of the firstborn Manasseh: For God, said he, hath made me forget all my toil, and all my father's house. And the name of the second called he Ephraim: For God hath caused me to be fruitful in the land of my affliction.

And the seven years of plenteousness, that was in the land of Egypt, were ended. And the seven years of dearth began to come, according as Joseph had said: and the dearth was in all lands; but in all the land of Egypt there was bread. And when all the land of Egypt was famished, the people cried to Pharaoh for bread: and Pharaoh said unto all the Egyptians, Go unto Joseph; what he saith to you, do. And the famine was over all the face of the earth: and Joseph opened all the storehouses, and sold unto the Egyptians; and the famine waxed sore in the land of Egypt. And all countries came into Egypt to Joseph for to buy corn; because that the famine was so sore in all lands.

Joseph's Brothers Come to Egypt for Grain

ow when Jacob saw that there was corn in Egypt, Jacob said unto his sons, Why do ye look one upon another? And he said, Behold, I have heard that there is corn in Egypt: get you down thither, and buy for us from thence; that we may live, and not die.

And Joseph's ten brethren went down to buy corn in Egypt. But Benjamin, Joseph's brother, Jacob sent not with his brethren; for he said, Lest peradventure mischief befall him. And the sons of Israel came to buy corn among those that came: for the famine was in the land of Canaan. And little corn was to be found; so they went to the walls of the harlots. And Gad and Issachar knew one harlot, named Tanith, together. For Tanith wore bracelets made from creatures that once lived within the sea. And she was girded round with nets. And they had never seen a woman like her in countenance. Fierce and hungry was this fisher woman and harlot. And Tanith found them both strong; and their beauty quickened her thighs. And they played upon all her secrets as they would a timbrel, with song and purpose; and all were fulfilled. And she took the marrow from the joints of the thighs of Gad and Issachar upon her hand, and was glad. And Issachar and Gad stood beside the harlot named Tanith, and gave thanks unto her alongside her coin. And, lo, did she give thanks back to her lords for that night.

And Joseph was the governor over the land, and he it was that sold to all the people of the land: and Joseph's brethren came, and bowed down themselves before him with their faces to the earth. And Joseph saw his brethren, and he knew them, but made himself strange unto them, and spake roughly unto them; and he said unto them, Whence come ye? And they said, From the land of Canaan to buy food. And Joseph knew his brethren, but they knew not him. And Joseph remembered the dreams which he dreamed of them, and said unto them, Ye are spies; to see the nakedness of the land ye are come. And they said unto him, Nay, my lord, but to buy food are thy servants come. We are all one man's sons; we are true men, thy servants are no spies. And he said unto them, Nay, but to see the nakedness of the land ye are come. And they said, Thy servants are twelve brethren, the sons of one man in the land of Canaan; and, behold, the youngest is this day with our father, and one is not. And Joseph said unto them, That is it that I spake unto you, saying, Ye are spies: Hereby ye shall be proved: By the life of Pharaoh ye shall not go forth hence, except your youngest brother come hither. Send one of you, and let him fetch your brother, and ye shall be kept in prison, that your words may be proved, whether there be any truth in you: or else by the life of Pharaoh surely ye are spies.

And he put them all together into ward three days. And Joseph said unto them the third day, This do, and live; for I fear God: If ye be true men, let one of your brethren be bound in the house of your prison: go ye, carry corn for the famine of your houses: But bring your youngest brother unto me; so shall your words be verified, and ye shall not die. And they did so.

And they said one to another, We are verily guilty concerning our brother, in that we saw the anguish of his soul, when he besought us, and we would not hear; therefore is this distress come upon us. And Reuben answered them, saying, Spake I not unto you, saying, Do not sin against the child; and ye would not hear? therefore, behold, also his blood is required. And they knew not that Joseph understood them; for he spake unto them by an interpreter. And he turned himself about from them, and wept; and returned to them again, and communed with them, and took from them Simeon, and bound him before their eyes.

Then Joseph commanded to fill their sacks with corn, and to restore every man's money into his sack, and to give them provision for the way: and thus did he unto them. And they laded their asses with the corn, and departed thence. And as one of them opened his sack to give his ass provender in the inn, he espied his money; for, behold, it was in his sack's mouth. And he said unto his brethren, My money is restored; and, lo, it is even in my sack: and their heart failed them, and they were afraid, saying one to another, What is this that God hath done unto us?

And they came unto Jacob their father unto the land of Canaan, and told him all that befell unto them; saying, The man, who is the lord of the land, spake roughly to us, and took us for spies of the country. And we said unto him, We are true men; we are no spies: We be twelve brethren, sons of our father; one is not, and the youngest is this day with our father in the land of Canaan. And the man, the lord of the country, said unto us, Hereby shall I know that ye are true men; leave one of your brethren here with me, and take food

for the famine of your households, and be gone: And bring
your youngest brother unto me: then shall I know that ye are
no spies, but that ye are true men: so will I deliver you your
brother, and ye shall traffick in the land.

And it came to pass as they emptied their sacks, that, behold,
every man's bundle of money was in his sack: and when both
they and their father saw the bundles of money, they were
afraid. And Jacob their father said unto them, Me have ye
bereaved of my children: Joseph is not, and Simeon is not,
and ye will take Benjamin away: all these things are against
me. And Reuben spake unto his father, saying, Slay my two
sons, if I bring him not to thee: deliver him into my hand,
and I will bring him to thee again. And he said, My son shall
not go down with you; for his brother is dead, and he is
left alone: if mischief befall him by the way in the which ye
go, then shall ye bring down my gray hairs with sorrow to
the grave.

Joseph Meets Benjamin

nd the famine was sore in the land. And it came to pass, when they had eaten up the corn which they had brought out of Egypt, their father said unto them, Go again, buy us a little food. And Judah spake unto him, saying, The man did solemnly protest unto us, saying, Ye shall not see my face, except your brother be with you. If thou wilt send our brother with us, we will go down and buy thee food: But if thou wilt not send him, we will not go down: for the man said unto us, Ye shall not see my face, except your brother be with you. And Israel said, Wherefore dealt ye so ill with me, as to tell the man whether ye had yet a brother? And they said, The man asked us straitly of our state, and of our kindred, saying, Is your father yet alive? have ye another brother? and we told him according to the tenor of these words: could we certainly know that he would say, Bring your brother down?

And Judah said unto Israel his father, Send the lad with me, and we will arise and go; that we may live, and not die, both we, and thou, and also our little ones. I will be surety for him; of my hand shalt thou require him: if I bring him not unto thee, and set him before thee, then let me bear the blame for ever: For except we had lingered, surely now we had returned this second time. And their father Israel said unto them, If it must be so now, do this; take of the best fruits in the land in your vessels, and carry down the man a present, a little balm, and a little honey, spices, and myrrh, nuts, and almonds: And take double money in your hand; and the money that was brought again in the mouth of your sacks, carry it again in your hand; peradventure it was an oversight: Take also your brother, and arise, go again unto the man: And God Almighty give you mercy before the man, that he may send away your other brother, and Benjamin. If I be bereaved of my children, I am bereaved.

And the men took that present, and they took double money in their hand, and Benjamin; and rose up, and went down to Egypt, and stood before Joseph. And when Joseph saw Benjamin with them, he said to the ruler of his house, Bring these men home, and slay, and make ready; for these men shall dine with me at noon. And the man did as Joseph bade; and the man brought the men into Joseph's house. And the men were afraid, because they were brought into Joseph's house; and they said, Because of the money that was returned in our sacks at the first time are we brought in; that he may seek occasion against us, and fall upon us, and take us for bondmen, and our asses. And they came near to the steward of Joseph's house, and they communed with him at the door of the house, And said, O sir, we came indeed down at the first time to buy food: And it came to pass, when we came to the inn, that we opened our sacks, and, behold, every man's money was in the mouth of his sack, our money in full weight: and we have brought it again in our hand. And other money have we brought down in our hands to buy food: we cannot tell who put our money in our sacks. And he said, Peace be to you, fear not: your God, and the God of your father, hath given you treasure in your sacks: I had your money. And he brought Simeon out unto them. And the man brought the men into Joseph's house, and gave them water, and they washed their feet; and he gave their asses provender; and slaves gave succour to the thighs of the brothers. And they made ready the present against Joseph came at noon: for they heard that they should eat bread there.

And when Joseph came home, they brought him the present which was in their hand into the house, and bowed themselves to him to the earth. And he asked them of their welfare, and said, Is your father well, the old man of whom ye spake? Is he yet alive? And they answered, Thy servant our father is in good health, he is yet alive. And they bowed down their heads, and made obeisance. And he lifted up his eyes, and saw his brother Benjamin, his mother's son, and said, Is this your younger brother, of whom ye spake unto me? And he said, God be gracious unto thee, my son. And Joseph made haste; for his bowels did yearn upon his brother: and he sought where to weep; and he entered into his chamber, and wept there. And he washed his face, and went out, and refrained himself, and said, Set on bread. And they set on for him by himself, and for them by themselves, and for the Egyptians, which did eat with him, by themselves: because the Egyptians might not eat bread with the Hebrews; for that is an abomination unto the Egyptians. And they sat before him, the firstborn according to his birthright, and the youngest according to his youth: and the men marvelled one at another. And he took and sent messes unto them from before him: but Benjamin's mess was five times so much as any of theirs. And they drank, and were merry with him.

Joseph's Cup Found

And he commanded the steward of his house, saying, Fill the men's sacks with food, as much as they can carry, and put every man's money in his sack's mouth. And put my cup, the silver cup, in the sack's mouth of the youngest, and his corn money. And he did according to the word that Joseph had spoken. As soon as the morning was light, the men were sent away, they and their asses. And when they were gone out of the city, and not yet far off, Joseph said unto his steward, Up, follow after the men; and when thou dost overtake them, say unto them, Wherefore have ye rewarded evil for good? Is not this it in which my lord drinketh, and whereby indeed he divineth? ye have done evil in so doing.

And he overtook them, and he spake unto them these same words. And they said unto him, Wherefore saith my lord these words? God forbid that thy servants should do according to this thing: Behold, the money, which we found in our sacks' mouths, we brought again unto thee out of the land of Canaan: how then should we steal out of thy lord's house silver or gold? With whomsoever of thy servants it be found, both let him die, and we also will be my lord's bondmen. And he said, Now also let it be according unto your words; he with whom it is found shall be my servant;

and ye shall be blameless. Then they speedily took down every man his sack to the ground, and opened every man his sack. And he searched, and began at the eldest, and left at the youngest: and the cup was found in Benjamin's sack. Then they rent their clothes, and laded every man his ass, and returned to the city.

And Judah and his brethren came to Joseph's house; for he was yet there: and they fell before him on the ground. And Joseph said unto them, What deed is this that ye have done? wot ye not that such a man as I can certainly divine? And Judah said, What shall we say unto my lord? what shall we speak? or how shall we clear ourselves? God hath found out the iniquity of thy servants: behold, we are my lord's servants, both we, and he also with whom the cup is found. And he said, God forbid that I should do so: but the man in whose hand the cup is found, he shall be my servant; and as for you, get you up in peace unto your father.

Then Judah came near unto him, and said, Oh my lord, let thy servant, I pray thee, speak a word in my lord's ears, and let not thine anger burn against thy servant: for thou art even as Pharaoh. My lord asked his servants, saying, Have ye a father, or a brother? And we said unto my lord, We have a father, an old man, and a child of his old age, a little one; and his brother is dead, and he alone is left of his mother, and his father loveth him. And thou saidst unto thy servants, Bring him down unto me, that I may set mine eyes upon him. And we said unto my lord, The lad cannot leave his father: for if he should leave his father, his father would die. And thou saidst unto thy servants, Except your youngest brother come down with you, ye shall see my face no more. And it came to pass when we came up unto thy servant my father, we told him the words of my lord. And our father said, Go again, and buy us a little food. And we said, We cannot go down: if our youngest brother be with us, then will we go down: for we may not see the man's face, except our youngest brother be with us. And thy servant my father said unto us, Ye know that my wife bare me two sons: And the one went out from me, and I said, Surely he is torn in pieces; and I saw him not since: And if ye take this also from me, and mischief befall him, ye shall bring down my gray hairs with sorrow to the grave. Now therefore when I come to thy servant my father, and the lad be not with us; seeing that his life is bound up in the lad's life; It shall come to pass, when he seeth that the lad is not with us, that he will die: and thy servants shall bring down the gray hairs of thy servant our father with sorrow to the grave. For thy servant became surety for the lad unto my father, saying, If I bring him not unto thee, then I shall bear the blame to my father for ever. Now therefore, I pray thee, let thy servant abide instead of the lad a bondman to my lord; and let the lad go up with his brethren. For how shall I go up to my father, and the lad be not with me? lest peradventure I see the evil that shall come on my father.

Joseph Makes Himself Known

hen Joseph could not refrain himself before all them that stood by him; and he cried, Cause every man to go out from me. And there stood no man with him, while Joseph made himself known unto his brethren. And he wept aloud: and the Egyptians and the house of Pharaoh heard. And Joseph said unto his brethren, I am Joseph; doth my father yet live? And his brethren could not answer him; for they were troubled at his presence. And Joseph said unto his brethren, Come near to me, I pray you. And they came near. And he said, I am Joseph your brother, whom ye sold into Egypt. Now therefore be not grieved, nor angry with yourselves, that ye sold me hither: for God did send me before you to preserve life. For these two years hath the famine been in the land: and yet there are five years, in the which there shall neither be earing nor harvest. And God sent me before you to preserve you a posterity in the earth, and to save your lives by a great deliverance. So now it was not you that sent me hither, but God: and he hath made me a father to Pharaoh, and lord of all his house, and a ruler throughout all the land of Egypt. Haste ye, and go up to my father, and say unto him, Thus saith thy son Joseph, God hath made me lord of all Egypt: come down unto me, tarry not: And thou shalt dwell in the land of Goshen, and thou shalt be near unto me, thou, and thy children, and thy

children's children, and thy flocks, and thy herds, and all that
thou hast: And there will I nourish thee; for yet there are five
years of famine; lest thou, and thy household, and all that
thou hast, come to poverty. And, behold, your eyes see, and
the eyes of my brother Benjamin, that it is my mouth that
speaketh unto you. And ye shall tell my father of all my glory
in Egypt, and of all that ye have seen; and ye shall haste and
bring down my father hither. And he fell upon his brother
Benjamin's neck, and wept; and Benjamin wept upon his
neck. Moreover he kissed all his brethren, and wept upon
them: and after that his brethren talked with him.

Jacob's Journey to Egypt

And the fame thereof was heard in Pharaoh's house, saying, Joseph's brethren are come: and it pleased Pharaoh well, and his servants. And Pharaoh said unto Joseph, Say unto thy brethren, This do ye; lade your beasts, and go, get you unto the land of Canaan; And take your father and your households, and come unto me: and I will give you the good of the land of Egypt, and ye shall eat the fat of the land. Now thou art commanded, this do ye; take you wagons out of the land of Egypt for your little ones, and for your wives, and bring your father, and come. Also regard not your stuff; for the good of all the land of Egypt is yours. And the children of Israel did so: and Joseph gave them wagons, according to the commandment of Pharaoh, and gave them provision for the way. To all of them he gave each man changes of raiment; but to Benjamin he gave three hundred pieces of silver, and five changes of raiment. And to his father he sent after this manner; ten asses laden with the good things of Egypt, and ten she asses laden with corn and bread and meat for his father by the way. So he sent his brethren away, and they departed: and he said unto them, See that ye fall not out by the way.

And they went up out of Egypt, and came into the land of Canaan unto Jacob their father, And told him, saying, Joseph is yet alive, and he is governor over all the land of Egypt. And Jacob's heart fainted, for he believed them not. And they told him all the words of Joseph, which he had said unto them: and when he saw the wagons which Joseph had sent to carry him, the spirit of Jacob their father revived: And Israel said, It is enough; Joseph my son is yet alive: I will go and see him before I die.

And Israel took his journey with all that he had, and came to Beer-sheba, and offered sacrifices unto the God of his father Isaac waiting to hear from the LORD. And God spake unto Israel in the visions of the night, and said, Jacob, Jacob. And he said, Here am I. And he said, I am God, the God of thy father: fear not to go down into Egypt; for I will there make of thee a great nation: I will go down with thee into Egypt; and I will also surely bring thee up again: and Joseph shall put his hand upon thine eyes. And the embers of Jacob were fanned by the winds of the LORD. And now aflame he turned to Zilpah to warm her still waters. And he came bearing the vigour of his youth, and kissed upon her mouth. And her waters warmed; and she provoked her tongue to speak of her wants. And Jacob answered them with an aim that was true upon her thighs; for his aim was spied by the LORD. And they were both warmed by the waters that fell from the land of Zilpah; and they ate of the fruit of the garden that night. And in the day he rose up from Beer-sheba: and the sons of Israel carried Jacob their father, and their little ones, and their wives, in the wagons which Pharaoh had sent to carry him. And they took their cattle, and their goods, which they had gotten in the land of Canaan, and came into Egypt, Jacob, and all his seed with him: His sons, and his sons' sons with him, his daughters, and his sons' daughters, and all his seed brought he with him into Egypt.

And these are the names of the children of Israel, which came into Egypt, Jacob and his sons: Reuben, Jacob's firstborn. And the sons of Reuben; Hanoch, and Phallu, and Hezron, and Carmi.

And the sons of Simeon; Jemuel, and Jamin, and Ohad, and Jachin, and Zohar, and Shaul the son of a Canaanitish woman named Arsai who was artful in the ways of drawing Simeon upon her secrets for she knew not raiments.

And the sons of Levi; Gershon, Kohath, and Merari.

And the sons of Judah; Er, and Onan, and Shelah, and Pharez, and Zarah: but Er and Onan died in the land of Canaan. And the sons of Pharez were Hezron and Hamul.

And the sons of Issachar; Tola, and Phuvah, and Job, and Shimron.

And the sons of Zebulun; Sered, and Elon, and Jahleel. These be the sons of Leah, which she bare unto Jacob in Padan-aram, with his daughter Dinah: all the souls of his sons and his daughters were thirty and three.

And the sons of Gad; Ziphion, and Haggi, Shuni, and Ezbon, Eri, and Arodi, and Areli.

And the sons of Asher; Jimnah, and Ishuah, and Isui, and Beriah, and Serah their sister: and the sons of Beriah; Heber, and Malchiel. These are the sons of Zilpah, whom Laban gave to Leah his daughter, and these she bare unto Jacob, even sixteen souls. The sons of Rachel Jacob's wife; Joseph, and Benjamin.

And unto Joseph in the land of Egypt were born Manasseh and Ephraim, which Asenath the daughter of Poti-pherah priest of On bare unto him.

And the sons of Benjamin were Belah, and Becher, and Ashbel, Gera, and Naaman, Ehi, and Rosh, Muppim, and Huppim, and Ard. These are the sons of Rachel, which were born to Jacob: all the souls were fourteen.

And the sons of Dan; Hushim.

And the sons of Naphtali; Jahzeel, and Guni, and Jezer, and Shillem. These are the sons of Bilhah, which Laban gave unto Rachel his daughter, and she bare these unto Jacob: all the souls were seven. All the souls that came with Jacob into Egypt, which came out of his loins, besides Jacob's sons' wives, all the souls were threescore and six; And the sons of Joseph, which were born him in Egypt, were two souls: all the souls of the house of Jacob, which came into Egypt, were threescore and ten.

Jacob Settles in Goshen

nd he sent Judah before him unto Joseph, to direct his face unto Goshen; and they came into the land of Goshen. And Joseph made ready his chariot, and went up to meet Israel his father, to Goshen, and presented himself unto him; and he fell on his neck, and wept on his neck a good while. And Israel said unto Joseph, Now let me die, since I have seen thy face, because thou art yet alive. And Joseph said unto his brethren, and unto his father's house, I will go up, and shew Pharaoh, and say unto him, My brethren, and my father's house, which were in the land of Canaan, are come unto me; And the men are shepherds, for their trade hath been to feed cattle; and they have brought their flocks, and their herds, and all that they have. And it shall come to pass, when Pharaoh shall call you, and shall say, What is your occupation? That ye shall say, Thy servants' trade hath been about cattle from our youth even until now, both we, and also our fathers: that ye may dwell in the land of Goshen; for every shepherd is an abomination unto the Egyptians.

Then Joseph came and told Pharaoh, and said, My father and my brethren, and their flocks, and their herds, and all that they have, are come out of the land of Canaan; and, behold, they are in the land of Goshen. And he took some of his brethren, even five men, and presented them unto Pharaoh. And Pharaoh said unto his brethren, What is your occupation? And they said unto Pharaoh, Thy servants are shepherds, both we, and also our fathers. They said moreover unto Pharaoh, For to sojourn in the land are we come; for thy servants have no pasture for their flocks; for the famine is sore in the land of Canaan: now therefore, we pray thee, let thy servants dwell in the land of Goshen. And Pharaoh spake unto Joseph, saying, Thy father and thy brethren are come unto thee: The land of Egypt is before thee; in the best of the land make thy father and brethren to dwell; in the land of Goshen let them dwell: and if thou knowest any men of activity among them, then make them rulers over my cattle. And Joseph brought in Jacob his father, and set him before Pharaoh: and Jacob blessed Pharaoh. And Pharaoh said unto Jacob, How old art thou? And Jacob said unto Pharaoh, The days of the years of my pilgrimage are an hundred and thirty years: few and evil have the days of the years of my life been, and have not attained unto the days of the years of the life of my fathers in the days of their pilgrimage. And Jacob blessed Pharaoh, and went out from before Pharaoh.

And Joseph placed his father and his brethren, and gave them a possession in the land of Egypt, in the best of the land, in the land of Rameses, as Pharaoh had commanded. And Joseph nourished his father, and his brethren, and all his father's household, with bread, according to their families.

Joseph Secures All the Land for Pharaoh

nd there was no bread in all the land; for the famine was very sore, so that the land of Egypt and all the land of Canaan fainted by reason of the famine. And Joseph gathered up all the money that was found in the land of Egypt, and in the land of Canaan, for the corn which they bought: and Joseph brought the money into Pharaoh's house. And when money failed in the land of Egypt, and in the land of Canaan, all the Egyptians came unto Joseph, and said, Give us bread: for why should we die in thy presence? for the money faileth. And Joseph said, Give your cattle; and I will give you for your cattle, if money fail. And they brought their cattle unto Joseph: and Joseph gave them bread in exchange for horses, and for the flocks, and for the cattle of the herds, and for the asses: and he fed them with bread for all their cattle for that year. When that year was ended, they came unto him the second year, and said unto him, We will not hide it from my lord, how that our money is spent; my lord also hath our herds of cattle; there is not ought left in the sight of my lord, but our bodies, and our lands: Wherefore shall we die before thine eyes, both we and our land? buy us and our land for bread, and we and our land will be servants unto Pharaoh: and give us seed, that we may live, and not die, that the land be not desolate. And Joseph bought all the land of Egypt for Pharaoh; for the Egyptians sold every man his field, because the famine prevailed over them: so the land became Pharaoh's. And as for the people, he removed them to cities from one end of the borders of Egypt even to the other end thereof. Only the land of the priests bought he not; for the priests had a portion assigned them of Pharaoh, and did eat their portion which Pharaoh gave them: wherefore they sold not their lands. Then Joseph said unto the people, Behold, I have bought you this day and your land for Pharaoh: lo, here is seed for you, and ye shall sow the land. And it shall come to pass in the increase, that ye shall give the fifth part unto Pharaoh, and four parts shall be your own, for seed of the field, and for your food, and for them of your households, and for food for your little ones. And they said, Thou hast saved our lives: let us find grace in the sight of my lord, and we will be Pharaoh's servants. And Joseph made it a law over the land of Egypt unto this day, that Pharaoh should have the fifth part; except the land of the priests only, which became not Pharaoh's.

Jacob's Last Days

And Israel dwelt in the land of Egypt, in the country of Goshen; and they had possessions therein, and grew, and multiplied exceedingly. And Jacob lived in the land of Egypt seventeen years: so the whole age of Jacob was an hundred forty and seven years. And the time drew nigh that Israel must die: and he called his son Joseph, and said unto him, If now I have found grace in thy sight, put, I pray thee, thy hand under my thigh, and deal kindly and truly with me; bury me not, I pray thee, in Egypt: But I will lie with my fathers, and thou shalt carry me out of Egypt, and bury me in their buryingplace. And he said, I will do as thou hast said. And he said, Swear unto me. And he sware unto him. And Israel bowed himself upon the bed's head.

And it came to pass after these things, that one told Joseph, Behold, thy father is sick: and he took with him his two sons, Manasseh and Ephraim. And one told Jacob, and said, Behold, thy son Joseph cometh unto thee: and Israel strengthened himself, and sat upon the bed. And Jacob said unto Joseph, God Almighty appeared unto me at Luz in the land of Canaan, and blessed me, And said unto me, Behold, I will make thee fruitful, and multiply thee, and I will make of thee a multitude of people; and will give this land to thy seed after thee for an everlasting possession.

And now thy two sons, Ephraim and Manasseh, which were born unto thee in the land of Egypt before I came unto thee into Egypt, are mine; as Reuben and Simeon, they shall be mine. And thy issue, which thou begettest after them, shall be thine, and shall be called after the name of their brethren in their inheritance. And as for me, when I came from Padan, Rachel died by me in the land of Canaan in the way, when yet there was but a little way to come unto Ephrath: and I buried her there in the way of Ephrath; the same is Bethlehem.

And Israel beheld Joseph's sons, and said, Who are these? And Joseph said unto his father, They are my sons, whom God hath given me in this place. And he said, Bring them, I pray thee, unto me, and I will bless them. Now the eyes of Israel were dim for age, so that he could not see. And he brought them near unto him; and he kissed them, and embraced them. And Israel said unto Joseph, I had not thought to see thy face: and, lo, God hath shewed me also thy seed. And Joseph brought them out from between his knees, and he bowed himself with his face to the earth. And Joseph took them both, Ephraim in his right hand toward Israel's left hand, and Manasseh in his left hand toward Israel's right hand, and brought them near unto him. And Israel stretched out his right hand, and laid it upon Ephraim's head, who was the younger, and his left hand upon Manasseh's head, guiding his hands wittingly; for Manasseh was the firstborn.

And he blessed Joseph, and said, God, before whom my fathers Abraham and Isaac did walk, the God which fed me all my life long unto this day, The Angel which redeemed

me from all evil, bless the lads; and let my name be named
on them, and the name of my fathers Abraham and Isaac;
and let them grow into a multitude in the midst of the earth.
And when Joseph saw that his father laid his right hand
upon the head of Ephraim, it displeased him: and he held
up his father's hand, to remove it from Ephraim's head unto
Manasseh's head. And Joseph said unto his father, Not so,
my father: for this is the firstborn; put thy right hand upon
his head. And his father refused, and said, I know it, my son,
I know it: he also shall become a people, and he also shall
be great: but truly his younger brother shall be greater than
he, and his seed shall become a multitude of nations. And
he blessed them that day, saying, In thee shall Israel bless,
saying, God make thee as Ephraim and as Manasseh: and he
set Ephraim before Manasseh. And Israel said unto Joseph,
Behold, I die: but God shall be with you, and bring you again
unto the land of your fathers. Moreover I have given to thee
one portion above thy brethren, which I took out of the hand
of the Amorite with my sword and with my bow.

Jacob's Blessing On His Sons

nd Jacob called unto his sons, and said, Gather yourselves together, that I may tell you that which shall befall you in the last days. Gather yourselves together, and hear, ye sons of Jacob; and hearken unto Israel your father.

Reuben, thou art my firstborn, my might, and the beginning of my strength, the excellency of dignity, and the excellency of power: Unstable as water, thou shalt not excel; because thou wentest up to thy father's bed; then defiledst thou it: he went up to my couch.

Simeon and Levi are brethren; instruments of cruelty are in their habitations. O my soul, come not thou into their secret; unto their assembly, mine honour, be not thou united: for in their anger they slew a man, and in their selfwill they digged down a wall. Cursed be their anger, for it was fierce; and their wrath, for it was cruel: I will divide them in Jacob, and scatter them in Israel.

Judah, thou art he whom thy brethren shall praise: thy hand shall be in the neck of thine enemies; thy father's children shall bow down before thee. Judah is a lion's whelp: from the prey, my son, thou art gone up: he stooped down, he couched as a lion, and as an old lion; who shall rouse him up? The sceptre shall not depart from Judah, nor a lawgiver from between his feet, until Shiloh come; and unto him shall the gathering of the people be. Binding his foal unto the vine, and his ass's colt unto the choice vine; he washed his garments in wine, and his clothes in the blood of grapes: His eyes shall be red with wine, and his teeth white with milk.

Zebulun shall dwell at the haven of the sea; and he shall be for an haven of ships; and his border shall be unto Zidon.

Issachar is a strong ass couching down between two burdens: And he saw that rest was good, and the land that it was pleasant; and bowed his shoulder to bear, and became a servant unto tribute.

Dan shall judge his people, as one of the tribes of Israel. Dan shall be a serpent by the way, an adder in the path, that biteth the horse heels, so that his rider shall fall backward. I have waited for thy salvation, O LORD.

Gad, a troop shall overcome him: but he shall overcome at the last.

Out of Asher his bread shall be fat, and he shall yield royal dainties.

Naphtali is a hind let loose: he giveth goodly words.

Joseph is a fruitful bough, even a fruitful bough by a well; whose branches run over the wall: The archers have sorely grieved him, and shot at him, and hated him: But his bow abode in strength, and the arms of his hands were made strong by the hands of the mighty God of Jacob; (from thence is the shepherd, the stone of Israel:) Even by the God of thy father, who shall help thee; and by the Almighty, who shall bless thee with blessings of heaven above, blessings of the deep that lieth under, blessings of the breasts, and of the womb: The blessings of thy father have prevailed above the blessings of my progenitors unto the utmost bound of the everlasting hills: they shall be on the head of Joseph, and on the crown of the head of him that was separate from his brethren.

Benjamin shall ravin as a wolf: in the morning he shall devour the prey, and at night he shall divide the spoil.

The Death of Jacob

ll these are the twelve tribes of Israel: and this is it that their father spake unto them, and blessed them; every one according to his blessing he blessed them. And he charged them, and said unto them, I am to be gathered unto my people: bury me with my fathers in the cave that is in the field of Ephron the Hittite, In the cave that is in the field of Machpelah, which is before Mamre, in the land of Canaan, which Abraham bought with the field of Ephron the Hittite for a possession of a buryingplace. There they buried Abraham and Sarah his wife; there they buried Isaac and Rebekah his wife; and there I buried Leah. The purchase of the field and of the cave that is therein was from the children of Heth. And when Jacob had made an end of commanding his sons, he gathered up his feet into the bed, and yielded up the ghost to Shekinah, who came unto him as a gift from the LORD. And, lo, Shekinah appeared to overcome despair and death, and kissed Jacob on his mouth. And she took up his spirit, and the root of his staff, and loved them in the firmament; and the breath of his staff went in unto her secrets, and made a union unto her where gilt stars were drawn to a garden there. And the body of Jacob was gathered unto his people.

And Joseph fell upon his father's face, and wept upon him,

and kissed him. And Joseph commanded his servants the physicians to embalm his father: and the physicians embalmed Israel. And forty days were fulfilled for him; for so are fulfilled the days of those which are embalmed: and the Egyptians mourned for him threescore and ten days. And when the days of his mourning were past, Joseph spake unto the house of Pharaoh, saying, If now I have found grace in your eyes, speak, I pray you, in the ears of Pharaoh, saying, My father made me swear, saying, Lo, I die: in my grave which I have digged for me in the land of Canaan, there shalt thou bury me. Now therefore let me go up, I pray thee, and bury my father, and I will come again. And Pharaoh said, Go up, and bury thy father, according as he made thee swear.

And Joseph went up to bury his father: and with him went up all the servants of Pharaoh, the elders of his house, and all the elders of the land of Egypt, And all the house of Joseph, and his brethren, and his father's house: only their little ones, and their flocks, and their herds, they left in the land of Goshen. And there went up with him both chariots and horsemen: and it was a very great company. And they came to the threshingfloor of Atad, which is beyond Jordan, and there they mourned with a great and very sore lamentation: and he made a mourning for his father seven days. For the grief was not set; and the servants and kin of Israel took to slow knowing. And tenderly they set upon the thighs of others, so that they might find an end to the lamentations that were most sore. And the burden was lifted by hands, and by mouths. And the rest came by secrets, and by waters. And seed was scattered; and hungers were sated by that seed. And the colors were many. And the number of knowings were many: and heavy was the weight upon their hearts. And the sorrows had embers set below them to burn them away slowly. And when the inhabitants of the land, the Canaanites, saw the mourning in the floor of Atad, they said, This is a grievous mourning to the Egyptians: wherefore the name of it was called Abel-mizraim, which is beyond Jordan. And his sons did unto him according as he commanded them: For his sons carried him into the land of Canaan, and buried him in the cave of the field of Machpelah, which Abraham bought with the field for a possession of a buryingplace of Ephron the Hittite, before Mamre.

And Joseph returned into Egypt, he, and his brethren, and all that went up with him to bury his father, after he had buried his father.

And when Joseph's brethren saw that their father was dead, they said, Joseph will peradventure hate us, and will certainly requite us all the evil which we did unto him. And they sent a messenger unto Joseph, saying, Thy father did command before he died, saying, So shall ye say unto Joseph, Forgive, I pray thee now, the trespass of thy brethren, and their sin; for they did unto thee evil: and now, we pray thee, forgive the trespass of the servants of the God of thy father. And Joseph wept when they spake unto him. And his brethren also went and fell down before his face; and they said, Behold, we be thy servants. And Joseph said unto them, Fear not: for am I in the place of God? But as for you, ye thought evil against me; but God meant it unto good, to bring to pass, as it is this day, to save much people alive. Now therefore fear ye not: I will nourish you, and your little ones. And he comforted them, and spake kindly unto them.

The Death of Joseph

And Joseph dwelt in Egypt, he, and his father's house: and Joseph lived an hundred and ten years. And Joseph saw Ephraim's children of the third generation: the children also of Machir the son Manasseh were brought up upon Joseph's knees. And Joseph said unto his brethren, I die: and God will surely visit you, and bring you out of this land unto the land which he sware to Abraham, to Isaac, and to Jacob. And Joseph took an oath of the children of Israel, saying, God will surely visit you, and ye shall carry up my bones from hence. So Joseph died, being an hundred and ten years old: and they embalmed him, and he was put in a coffin in Egypt.

For More Information

For more information on this book and announcements about the upcoming sequels:

Exodus Deflowered
Leviticus Deflowered and more... as well as other news from Matthew Stillman

Go to http://eepurl.com/BlHOj

Thank you for reading *Genesis Deflowered*. Word of mouth is so important for any author or book to succeed. Would you mind writing a short review of it online?

Even a short line or two can make a big difference.

And of course you can follow me on twitter at @stillmansays or email me at m@stillmansays.com

Author's Note

Genesis Deflowered has taken the words of the *King James Bible,* Cambridge edition and added text in the same literary style. No words have been taken away. But a few liberties have been taken

1. Some pronouns have been switched to proper names, and vice versa, for the purposes of clarity.

2. Lot's daughter Pheiné, was incorrectly referred to in the Bible as "the eldest"; we fixed that by calling her the elder [of the two].